"Who the hell are Lily Cunningham.

"A rich dilettante killing a few months in a backwater?"

She sucked in air like a drowning man. *"That's* what you think of me?"

"Am I wrong?"

"Only totally." Planting both hands on his broad chest, she gave him a mighty shove that, much to her disgust, didn't budge him an inch. "You are a completely infuriating man."

"That's been said before."

"Hardly surprising." Liliy whirled around and took two quick steps.

Ron dropped one big hand on her shoulder. "Running away?"

"I do not run away from anything."

"Then what's your hurry?"

She took a long, deep breath and prayed for patience. "Tell me why I should stand here and let you insult me in my own office."

He looked down at her and held her gaze. Then he said, softly, unexpectedly, "I don't want you to go."

Dear Reader,

Well, it's that time of year again—and if those beautiful buds of April are any indication, you're in the mood for love! And what better way to sustain that mood than with our latest six Special Edition novels? We open the month with the latest installment of Sherryl Woods's MILLION DOLLAR DESTINIES series, *Priceless*. When a pediatric oncologist who deals with life and death on a daily basis meets a sick child's football hero, she thinks said hero can make the little boy's dreams come true. But little does she know that he can make hers a reality, as well! Don't miss this compelling story....

MERLYN COUNTY MIDWIVES continues with Maureen Child's *Forever...Again*, in which a man who doesn't believe in second chances has a change of mind—not to mention heart—when he meets the beautiful new public relations guru at the midwifery clinic. In *Cattleman's Heart* by Lois Faye Dyer, a businesswoman assigned to help a struggling rancher finds that business is the last thing on her mind when she sees the shirtless cowboy meandering toward her! And Susan Mallery's popular DESERT ROGUES are back! In *The Sheik & the Princess in Waiting*, a woman learns that the man she loved in college has two secrets: 1) he's a prince; and 2) they're married! Next, can a pregnant earthy vegetarian chef find happiness with town's resident playboy, an admitted carnivore... and father of her child? Find out in *The Best of Both Worlds* by Elissa Ambrose. And in Vivienne Wallington's *In Her Husband's Image*, a widow confronted with her late husband's twin brother is forced to decide, as she looks in the eyes of her little boy, if some secrets are worth keeping.

So enjoy the beginnings of spring, and all six of these wonderful books! And don't forget to come back next month for six new compelling reads from Silhouette Special Edition.

Happy reading!

Gail Chasan
Senior Editor

Please address questions and book requests to:
Silhouette Reader Service
U.S.: 3010 Walden Ave., P.O. Box 1325, Buffalo, NY 14269
Canadian: P.O. Box 609, Fort Erie, Ont. L2A 5X3

Forever...Again

MAUREEN CHILD

Silhouette

SPECIAL EDITION

Published by Silhouette Books

America's Publisher of Contemporary Romance

To Cherry Adair, for helping me
find the writing magic…again.

SILHOUETTE BOOKS

ISBN 0-373-24604-8

FOREVER…AGAIN

Visit Silhouette at www.eHarlequin.com

Printed in U.S.A.

Books by Maureen Child

Silhouette Special Edition

Forever…Again #1604

Silhouette Desire

Have Bride, Need Groom #1059
*The Surprise Christmas
   Bride* #1112
Maternity Bride #1138
*The Littlest Marine #1167
**The Non-Commissioned
   Baby* #1174
*The Oldest Living Married Virgin #1180
*Colonel Daddy #1211
*Mom in Waiting #1234
*Marine under the Mistletoe #1258
*The Daddy Salute #1275
*The Last Santini Virgin #1312
*The Next Santini Bride #1317
*Marooned with a Marine #1325
*Prince Charming in Dress Blues #1366
*His Baby! #1377
*The Last Virgin in California #1398
Did You Say Twins?! #1408
The SEAL's Surrender #1431
*The Marine & the Debutante #1443
The Royal Treatment #1468
Kiss Me, Cowboy! #1490
Beauty & the Blue Angel #1514
Sleeping with the Boss #1534
Man Beneath the Uniform #1561

*Bachelor Battalion

Silhouette Books

Love Is Murder
"In Too Deep"

Harlequin Historicals

Shotgun Grooms #575
"Jackson's Mail-Order Bride"

MAUREEN CHILD

is a California native who loves to travel. Every chance they get, she and her husband are taking off on another research trip. The author of more than sixty books, Maureen loves a happy ending and still swears that she has the best job in the world. She lives in Southern California with her husband, two children and a golden retriever with delusions of grandeur.

Visit her Web site at www.maureenchild.com.

Merlyn County Regional
Hospital Happenings

Congratulations to midwife Milla Johnson on her engagement to our very own handsome pediatrician, Dr. Kyle Bingham! With two such wonderful people on our staff, the children of Merlyn County couldn't be in better hands! A bridal shower for the happy couple is in the works. Please see the receptionist's desk for more details.

Detective Bryce Collins is still working alongside Dr. Mari Bingham on the investigation into procedures at the Foster Clinic. Please give the detective your full cooperation should he request information about the hospital. And please continue to report *any* strange behavior at the Foster Clinic or in the pharmacy department to Dr. Bingham or her receptionist.

Volunteers for PR director Lily Cunningham's next great fund-raising idea should contact the receptionist's desk. (And anyone who sees CEO Ron Bingham hanging around Lily's office and grumbling about the festivities—ignore him!)

Chapter One

Lily Cunningham laughed to herself as she swiped a paper towel along the counter in one of the birthing rooms. If her friends in New York could see her now, she thought. They'd never believe it. But then who would?

A woman of forty-five who'd hit the top of her profession, made tons of money and lived in a plush apartment in Manhattan would appear to have everything she'd ever wanted. Right?

Wrong.

Lily crumpled the paper towel, stepped on the pedal of the gleaming stainless steel trash can and dropped the used paper inside. Smiling to herself, she left the birthing room, turning the light out behind her.

Stepping into the hall, she breathed deeply, enjoying the cool, soothing pastel tones on the walls and the scent of fresh flowers drifting through the women's clinic. The sound of the three-inch heels of her scarlet pumps were muffled on the carpeted hallway as she made her way to her office. Smiling and nodding at the people she passed, she heard the indignant cry of a newborn from one room, and from behind the closed door of another, she heard a midwife calmly saying, "You have to remember to breathe, Shelley."

Lily smiled and kept walking.

This is what made her happy, she thought.

Being here.

In Kentucky.

At the Foster Midwifery Clinic.

Doing work that meant something. That had impact on people's lives. That required more of her than looking spectacular at a business dinner.

"Lily!"

She stopped and swung around to face Mari Bingham, the wonderful doctor who'd brought Lily on as public relations director in the first place. As usual, Mari was walking at a half run. The woman simply never slowed down.

"Where's the fire?" Lily asked, smiling.

"Where *isn't* a fire?" Mari shook her head and then jammed both hands into the pockets of her white lab coat, rummaging around in their depths. "I swear, it's as if the whole county decided nine months ago that it would be a great time to make a baby."

"I noticed." And Lily liked it. She'd never had children of her own, which was just one of the small sore spots that ached in the corners of her heart. Oh, she'd learned to live with the disappointment years ago, and being here, constantly in the midst of labors and deliveries...almost made her feel a part of everything.

Working for the midwifery clinic and women's ealth center was like having a ringside seat for a miracle, every day.

"We've only got the one birthing room empty at the moment." Lily grinned. "If this keeps up, maybe you should think about expanding."

Mari's eyes widened. "Bite your tongue," she said on a half laugh. "We've got plenty to do right now, with the clinic and the..." Her voice trailed off and a scowl tightened her expression.

Lily could have kicked herself. She hadn't meant to give Mari any reason to think about the ridiculous accusations flying around. But judging by the tired, haunted look in Mari's eyes, the younger woman was doing a lot of thinking lately, with or without Lily's reminders.

Reaching out, she laid one hand on Mari's arm, and the woman stilled. "You're not to worry about any of this, you know," Lily said. "It's bull, all of it. And that sheriff will figure it out sooner or later."

Mari sighed and at last pulled her right hand free of her pocket, a slip of paper clutched in her hand. "I've known Bryce practically my whole life," she said softly. Shaking her head, she shifted her gaze from Lily's as if she couldn't bear to meet the sympathy and understanding she'd find there. "If someone had told me a few months ago that I'd be his prime suspect in an illegal drug investigation, I'd have laughed myself sick."

"As you should," Lily said.

"It doesn't sound so funny anymore." Mari glanced over her shoulder, down the long hallway toward the waiting room. Sitting in chairs were a half-dozen women waiting to be examined. Small children sat at the miniature tables and chairs, reading books or coloring. Everything looked perfectly normal. And it really wasn't. Nothing had been normal in months.

Turning around, Mari lifted her gaze to Lily's. "If Bryce doesn't clear this up soon, we may lose even more funding, and then I don't know what we'll do."

"That's for *me* to worry about," Lily said firmly, making sure her voice sounded way more confident than she felt at the moment. "You'll see. The fund-raising party will bring in bushel loads of cash. We'll leave our important guests staggered and, hopefully, broke."

Mari smiled and nodded, though doubt flickered in her eyes.

"Nice thought. And on that subject—" Mari held out the slip of paper "—this is why I stopped you. It's the name and number of another possible contributor. My grandmother says, and I quote, 'They've got more money than sense, honey. They should be good for a sizable donation.'"

"Your grandmother should have my job."

"Oh, no." Mari smiled and this time her heart was in it. "Grandmother doesn't have the kind of tact required to part a billionaire from his wallet."

"And that's where I come in." Lily grinned and winked. She snatched the piece of paper. "You'll see, Mari. Everything is going to be fine."

"Your mouth to God's ear."

"Oh," Lily smiled and promised, *"always."*

As Mari hurried back down the long, well-lit hall, Lily stared after her. Despite waving her pom-poms for Mari's sake, Lily was a little worried. Things had just been so darn strange lately. She never would have expected to run into a drug scandal in a small town in Kentucky. But then, she thought wearily, some things know no boundaries.

Turning back toward her office, she walked inside, sat down behind her desk and took a moment to admire her surroundings. Always a woman who preferred beauty whenever possible, she'd painted her office walls a soft, dreamy blue, and had hung white, lacy curtains at the windows. Framed watercolors—some by local artists—hung on the walls, and two crystal vases held cheerful bouquets of simple flowers. The daisies, carnations and peonies brightened the room, and their combined fragrance scented the air like summer perfume. A Bokhara rug in shades of crimson and gold covered the plain, serviceable carpet and was the perfect backdrop for her Queen Anne desk.

Naturally, most of the other offices at the clinic weren't quite so lavishly appointed. But Lily was a big believer in making your workspace comfortable. If she enjoyed pretty things, why shouldn't she bring them in to brighten up her office?

A china tea service sat on the library table beneath the window, where sunlight dazzled through the lacy sheers to form dainty patterns across the carpet. Easing back in her maroon leather chair, Lily toed her heels off, lifted her legs and propped her feet on the corner of her desk. She wiggled her toes and nearly sighed at the relief. Fashion could be a killer, she mused.

Lifting one hand to push her hair back from her

face, she set the charms on her heavy, platinum bracelet jangling.

"I always know when you're around," a deep
voice said from the open doorway, "you're like a cat
with a bell around its neck."

Lily's stomach jumped and she almost pulled her
feet down off the desk, but just managed to stop herself. What would be the point of pretending dignity
when the man had already seen her?

Ron Bingham, Mari's father, and currently the
thorn in Lily's side, took up most of the doorway.
Leaning his right shoulder against the jamb, he stared
at her as if he had all the time in the world.

Sharp, blue-green eyes bored into hers from across
the room. His neat black hair was lightly sprinkled
with gray at the temples, and he wore a flawlessly
groomed beard and mustache. She'd never been a fan
of beards, but as beards went, she had to admit Ron's
was handsome. He wore a pair of neatly pressed khaki
slacks, dark-brown dress shoes and a starched-within-
an-inch-of-its-life white, long-sleeved shirt. His tan
jacket actually had suede patches at the elbows, and
his solemn brown tie finished off the image of suc-
cessful and yet somehow *boring* business man.

Although, she thought, despite his dismal taste in
clothing, Ron Bingham could never *actually* be considered boring. He was far too irritating for that.

Lily propped her elbows on the arms of her chair

and hoped her sleek, red skirt wasn't drooping enough to give him a view of anything interesting. "So, you knew I'd be here because of the sound of my charm bracelet?"

"Yep."

One-word answers.

So caveman.

So annoying.

And why, in this man, so attractive?

"Well," Lily said, smiling, "aren't you the world-class detective? Most people would have assumed I was here because of my name on the door."

His lips twitched, but he didn't look any too happy about it.

"Clever woman."

"Thank you."

"Never cared for *clever* women."

"Well," Lily said, "color me crushed."

He sighed and pushed away from the door. Folding his arms across an impressively broad chest, he tipped his head to one side and stared at her. "Is there any reason in particular we seem to swipe at each other all the time?"

"Because it's fun?" Lily smiled, enjoying his discomfort. She supposed she should feel badly about that, but really, the man was so stuffy, he probably just stood his suits up in the corner every night rather than bothering with a closet. How he ever could have fathered a daughter as charming and sweet natured as Mari was simply beyond her. His late wife must have had all the charisma in the family gene pool.

Ron Bingham stared down at her and wondered why the hell he bothered. Why was it he always felt compelled to stop by this woman's office when he was at the clinic? Why did he always allow himself to be drawn into a baiting contest?

Lillith, Lily, Cunningham was exactly the kind of woman he'd always avoided. Born into a wealthy family and living the kind of privileged life most people could only dream about, she appeared to trip through life with a studied indifference that simply confounded him. She had no *plan.* She had no work ethic. She had no…she had no business wearing bright red suits with short skirts and high heels that totally distracted a perfectly sane man.

When Mari first hired Lily as the new PR director for the clinic, Ron had expected to dislike the woman on sight. He'd assumed she'd roar into this tiny corner of Kentucky and proclaim it backwoodsy. Instead, she was dropping seamlessly into life here and, damn it, doing a good job with the clinic as well. Which only served to heighten his confusion.

"To what do I owe the honor of this visit?" she asked, and he hated that he noticed the deep timbre of her voice.

Telling himself to stop acting like a dumbstruck

teenager, Ron got a grip on his roving thoughts and spoke up. "I'm here to pick up the list of people you're inviting to the fund-raiser."

One blond eyebrow lifted into a delicate arch over her steady brown eyes. "You're a messenger now?"

He scowled at her. "Simply doing a favor."

Lily smiled then, and he tried not to notice the wattage in that simple act. But when the woman turned on the juice, her whole face lit up and her eyes seemed to sparkle.

"I know," she said. "Just teasing. Actually, I spoke to your mother this morning. I already sent a copy of the list to her."

Ron frowned and wondered why in the hell his mother hadn't bothered to tell him that this trip to the clinic was unnecessary. If he'd known, he could have stayed away and saved both himself and Lily the bother of yet another round in their game of one-upmanship.

She swung her legs off the edge of the desk in a graceful sweep that caught his attention despite his better judgment. But hell, he was male, wasn't he? Only natural that he should notice a pair of shapely legs. And as she slid her feet into the high heels that did absolutely amazing things for her calves, he told himself there was nothing unusual about *looking*. It was touching that he wouldn't—couldn't—allow himself.

Not that he *wanted* to touch.

He groaned inwardly and focused his gaze on her big brown eyes instead. He wasn't entirely sure which view was safer.

She stood up and her bold red suit seemed to cling to every curve. And, God help him, she had plenty of curves. She wasn't very tall, no more than five-six or -seven, but every inch of her was solidly packed.

"I can give you another copy if you like..."

"Not necessary," he said, already backing toward the door. *Coward* his brain whispered.

Damn right, he countered silently.

"If you're worried about the clinic, you needn't be," she said.

Instantly Ron's attention shifted to where it should, hopefully, remain. On business.

"You'll forgive me if I go ahead and worry anyway."

"Of course you will."

The sigh behind her words had him asking, "What's that supposed to mean?"

She eased one hip onto the corner of her desk, perching gingerly against the antique furniture. "I only meant that people like you will worry whether there's cause or not."

"People like *me?*"

She lifted her left hand into a brief wave, and that

bracelet of hers chimed musically. "You know, stuffy, stalwart types."

Stalwart he could live with. Stuffy seemed a little...insulting.

"And you figure you know my 'type' quite well, do you?"

"Not hard to guess."

Leave now, he thought. Leave before you get drawn into yet another contest of wills with a woman who had absolutely no "back-up gear" in her. Naturally though, he couldn't do that.

"I'm fascinated," he said dryly.

She smiled briefly. "Oh, I can see that."

"Please, explain my 'type.'"

She paused, watching him, and even the air between them hummed with expectation. Then she started talking.

"Okay..." She pushed off the desk and walked across her ridiculously expensive and out-of-place rug to stop just inches in front of him. "I grew up around people as sturdy as you, you know. So I speak from experience."

"Can't wait."

One corner of her mouth twitched, and his gaze fastened on the curve of her lip, damn it.

"You always do what's expected of you."

"And that's bad?"

"Just boring."

"And boring is a crime?"

"Just tedious."

"Oh," he said, giving her a slow nod, "do go on."

"All right." She walked a slow circle around him, and Ron could have sworn he felt her gaze sweep him up and down as if he were an interesting slide show in a biology class. "You make decisions based on what's best for 'the family.' Never any side trip into interesting…just a long, slow trip on the main highway. Go where you're supposed to be and get there in the prescribed manner."

He shifted position uncomfortably. She managed to make him sound like an automaton.

"And you prefer the side roads?"

"Of course." She shrugged.

"Don't you get lost?"

"See new territory, discover new things."

"And you don't believe in maps, then, either?"

"Maps." She shook her head. "They're for outlining the road, and what fun is that? You might as well stay at home and draw red lines on an atlas. If you're not open to discovery, why go at all?"

"Are we still talking about stodgy, stalwart lives or have we moved on to summer road trips?"

"I said 'stuffy' not 'stodgy'," she corrected. "And isn't life the same thing as a good road trip?"

"How do you figure?" Somehow he'd lost control of this conversation. That happened all too often around Lily Cunningham. She seemed to have her own sort of logic that defied description.

She stopped in front of him again and tipped her head back so that she was looking directly into his eyes. The soft scent of jasmine lifted from her hair, and before he could remind himself not to notice...he had.

"Everyone starts out on the same road. Some of us stay on the highway—some of us take the back roads." She smiled again. "Just like life. Some of us never look away from the goal long enough to be sure there isn't some other goal that would be just as good if not better. You miss a lot when you never get off the highway."

"Maybe," Ron said. "But you don't run into many dead ends that way, either."

Chapter Two

Ridiculous, but hours later Lily was still thinking about her conversation with Ron Bingham. There was simply something about the man. That could be good…or bad. But either way, he was spending far too much time in her thoughts.

Deliberately turning her mind away from him, Lily swung her leather bag over her shoulder and left her office for the day. Heading down the hall, she walked in step to the music drifting through the speakers. Passing through the waiting room, she smiled at a little boy holding up his scribbled drawing of what might have been a pony—if ponies were allowed six legs. Tired mothers and pregnant women still crowded the waiting room and Lily knew Mari wouldn't leave the building until every last one of them had been seen and reassured. The woman really was a wonder, Lily thought, admiration flaring.

Dr. Mari Bingham was determined to make the clinic her grandmother had founded the best of its kind. Even that, though, wasn't enough for Mari. The biomedical facility she wanted to build would not only bring needed jobs into Merlyn County, it would spearhead research into infertility and stem cells and other life-saving—though possibly controversial—areas.

Lily sighed as she stood in the center of the lobby and let her gaze drift from one woman to another as they read magazines or chatted. What were they thinking? Oh, she knew they'd come for prenatal care and that was all to the good. But Lily had also heard the talk flying around town. Gossip about Mari and her plans, and about the high-powered backers who'd pulled out their monetary support for the facility. There was just too much gossip, Lily thought. Of course, in a small town, you really couldn't avoid it. Still, one would think that the very women Mari was working so hard to serve would be willing to defend her rather than talk about her behind her back.

Mari worked like a dog to make sure the women in this part of Kentucky could have good prenatal care—and a clean, welcoming place in which to give birth, whether the women wanted to use a midwife or a doctor. But sometimes, Lily told herself, it was the people who owed you the most who enjoyed talking you down. Maybe people just didn't care to be beholden to anyone.

The chatter around her lifted and fell, then dropped away completely as she pushed through the glass door and stepped into the afternoon sunlight. The weather was close, as it had been all summer. Humidity made the air thick enough to chew. But beyond the misery of the heat, there was a clean freshness to the Kentucky mountain air that she'd never found anywhere else.

New York's crowded streets with their racing pedestrians and noisy cabs seemed a world away, and Lily was glad for it. She'd needed this change. This chance to step off the treadmill and enjoy her life a little. The work at the clinic was challenging enough to keep her happy—while giving her time to explore the new world she found herself in.

She'd only been in rural Kentucky a few months, but already it felt like home. Here, no one cared if she wanted to walk barefoot down Main Street. There were no reporters ready to snap a picture of Lillith Cunningham being anything less than dignified. And, there was enough of a buffer zone between her and her family that Lily felt free, for the first time in her life.

Two or three pickup trucks dotted the parking lot, alongside a couple of minivans and a station wagon that looked to be on its last legs. Sunlight speared from the sky and glanced off the asphalt until heat waves shimmered in the air.

"Like walking with a wet electric blanket wrapped around you," Lily muttered as she slipped out of her suit jacket and stepped out of her heels. The parking lot felt red hot against the soles of her feet and still it was more comfortable than walking another step on three-inch heels.

For all the problems crowding in on the clinic, Lily didn't for a moment regret moving here. Binghamton, Kentucky, was as far removed from New York City as the moon was from the sun. Everything was different here. Even *she* was different.

All right, maybe not so different. But at least here, Lily thought, her differences fit right in. Growing up in an "old money" family, she'd been the black sheep almost from the moment of her birth. Born in the family limousine on the *way* to the hospital, Lily had never lived down her "undignified" entrance into the world. In fact, she'd pretty much done all she could to live up to it.

In high school she'd dyed her hair purple, worn her skirts too short and dated all the "wrong" boys. She drove too fast, listened to what her parents called "appalling" music and took part in protest marches. By the time she left home for college, Lily could have sworn she could actually *hear* the stately old Boston family home breathe a sigh of relief. Heaven knew, her parents had.

At college things were different. At UCLA she'd discovered a whole new world. In California life was more relaxed, less rigid. There were fewer rules, and no one thought of wearing anything more formal than a pair of clean jeans. Lily had found a place where she fit in. She'd thrived on the distance from her caring, but stiffly formal family. She'd even fallen in love.

"But then," she muttered as she hit the button on her keychain that would unlock her car, "nothing's perfect."

Her marriage hadn't started out badly. Everything had been fine. Until the day a doctor told Lily she couldn't have children. And just like that, it was over. Jack was packed and gone within the week—the divorce was final six months later.

Lily opened her car door and tossed her purse across to the passenger seat. Tilting her face up, she looked at the cloud-scattered sky and blew out a breath. The past didn't matter anymore. Whatever paths she'd taken in her life, they'd eventually led her here. And that was all that mattered.

Sliding into her car, she jammed the key home, turned it and instantly flipped up the volume on her radio. An oldie but goodie came pouring out of the speakers and as Lily put the car in reverse, she started singing along.

She turned left out of the lot and headed toward downtown. In no rush to hurry home, she decided the heat of the day called for a reprieve. Driving to South Junction Burgers, she kept singing as she imagined getting her hands on one of the burger joint's famous milkshakes.

The air-conditioning hit her like a slap, and Lily almost reeled with the impact. The diner felt like heaven. Only a handful of customers were inside, and Lily smiled at them as she headed back to her favorite…and luckily empty booth.

She slid onto the worn Naugahyde and didn't even bother picking up one of the menus tucked between the sugar and the salt and pepper shakers. What would be the point? South Junction wasn't fine cuisine. People came here for one reason.

"Hey, Ms. Cunningham."

Lily smiled up at her waitress. "Hi, Vickie."

Vickie Hastings had a mountain of blond hair, pulled up on top of her head and then lacquered into complete submission. Her blue eyes were lined heavily with black eyeliner, and her mascara had been layered on so thickly, she looked as if two caterpillars were taking naps on her eyelids. She snapped her gum and wore her short uniform dress way too tight, across breasts she seemed inordinately proud of, but she had a nice smile and was always friendly.

"The usual?" Vickie asked, pulling her pad and pen from her apron pocket.

Lily laughed. Good God. She was a regular at a diner. Her mother would be hysterical. And that cheered Lily a little. "You bet. Only tonight, make the milkshake strawberry for a change."

Vickie chuckled. "I don't know. Living dangerously. If you don't have a chocolate shake on Thursday nights, the world might stop spinning."

"Let's risk it."

"You got it." Vickie filled out the order pad, but didn't move away.

"Is something wrong?"

"Well." The waitress threw a glance over her shoulder at the long counter behind her and the open pass-through to the kitchen where her boss was cooking. When she was assured no one was paying attention to her, she turned back to Lily and said, "Now that you mention it…"

The air-conditioning had done its job. Lily felt refreshed enough to handle whatever it was that had Vickie worrying her bottom lip. "What's wrong?"

"I'm uh—" she leaned in a little closer and lowered her voice "—pregnant."

Lily blinked. This kind of news wasn't usually delivered with all the stealth of a CIA man making a hand-off to his partner. "Congratulations?" she asked, unsure if Vickie was wanting to celebrate or commiserate.

"Thanks." A brief smile curved Vickie's mouth and then disappeared again a moment later. "Billy'n me're real happy about it. But the thing is," she leaned in even closer, and soon, Lily thought, the two of them would be nose to nose. "I was wondering. You work at the clinic."

"Yes…" A flicker of irritation started at the base of Lily's spine, and she told herself to fight it. She didn't know what Vickie was going to say so there was no point in getting angry or defensive.

Yet.

"I wanted to ask you if going in there is really safe."

There it was.

That tiny flicker of irritation became a flame and quickly jumped to an inferno as it climbed her spine, jittered her nerves and settled, unfortunately for Vickie, in Lily's mouth.

"For heaven's sake, Vickie!" Lily leaned back, but kept her gaze locked eyeball to eyeball with the younger woman. "You've known Mari Bingham all your life. And you can ask me something like that?"

Vickie's expression tightened, and a flash of what might have been shame darted across her eyes, but it was gone again in an instant, so it was hard to be sure. "I'm just askin'," she said, defending her right to badmouth an old friend. "There's been talk."

"There certainly has," Lily snapped, then belatedly remembered to keep her voice down. She shot a quick look around the diner, then focused her gaze on Vickie again. "And its being spread by people too foolish or too ignorant to know any better."

"Now, Ms. Cunningham…" Insulted, she straightened up.

"Oh no, you don't," Lily said, grabbing Vickie's hand as the woman started backing off. "You asked me a question and you're not leaving until you've had your answer."

But Vickie was obviously regretting saying anything. Her gaze darted around the room, and even Lily could see that Danny, the cook and owner, was watching them from the kitchen. It didn't stop her.

"Now, you listen to me, Vickie."

"Yes, ma'am."

"Mari Bingham is the most dedicated, caring, loving person I've ever known. She works harder than anyone I've ever seen and she's devoted herself to making sure you and every other woman in Merlyn County get the kind of care you deserve.''

''Yes.'' Anxious now, Vickie was willing to agree to anything as she tried to pull her hand free of Lily's grasp. She didn't succeed.

''Any problems that are going on have nothing to do with Mari or her clinic and you should be ashamed of yourself for even thinking that they do.''

''Ms. Cunningham…''

But Lily's temper was up and there was just no stopping her. Her voice dropped a notch, but none of the fury left it. ''Do you really believe for one *instant* that Mari Bingham is dealing *drugs?*''

Vickie sucked in a breath, clearly horrified. ''Course not, but—''

''No buts. Do you trust Mari? Do you know her?''

''Yes—''

''Then don't you think you've answered your own question, Vickie?''

''I guess so, but still there's—''

Lily's eyes narrowed and Vickie shut up fast, keeping whatever she'd been about to say to herself. Just as well, Lily thought. It would do no good to browbeat the populace of Binghamton one at a time. For heaven's sake, if they didn't believe in one of their own, how on earth could *she,* an outsider, convince them? And Lily had no illusions about her status. She could live in Binghamton for the next fifty years and she'd always be considered an outsider.

Taking a deep breath, she blew it out again quickly, then forced a smile she didn't feel and released her grip on Vickie's wrist. "I'm sorry," she said, giving the waitress's hand a belated pat. "I shouldn't have lost my temper."

"It's okay," Vickie admitted. "My Bill, he's always saying I'm enough to drive a saint right out of Heaven."

"Well," Lily said with a short laugh, "I'm no saint."

Vickie took an uneasy step backward but shared the laugh. "And the Junction sure isn't Heaven."

"Too true." Lily smoothed her hair back from her face, then calmly and coolly folded her hands together on the scarred tabletop. "So, I guess I'll be staying. Could I have that milkshake right away, Vickie. I think I could use a little cooling off."

"Right." She nodded. "I mean, yes, ma'am. Coming right up."

As the younger woman scurried back toward the counter, Lily sucked in another deep breath and told herself she was going to have to take it easy. It wouldn't help Mari's or the clinic's case at all if word got around that their PR director was running around town shouting at people who disagreed with her.

Damn it.

"That was well done."

The deep voice came from the booth directly behind her, and Lily stilled completely. Only one man she knew had a voice as deep and rumbling as that. And wouldn't you know he'd be sitting right behind her.

Shifting on the seat, she glanced over her shoulder and met Ron Bingham's steady gaze. Really, his eyes were more blue than green, but most of the time they were just the shade of the ocean.

Which had nothing to do with anything.

"I suppose you heard everything."

"You're not exactly a quiet woman, Ms. Cunningham."

She blew out an exasperated breath. "Do you have to do that?" she demanded.

"Do what?"

"Call me Ms. Cunningham."

One dark eyebrow lifted. "Your name, isn't it?"

"Yes, but I've been here several months, now. Don't you think you could break down and call me Lily?"

He leaned one arm on the seatback and stared at her. "Suppose I could."

"That's something, then." Deciding to ignore him and the fact that no matter where she went he seemed to pop up like the proverbial bad penny, she turned around again.

"Alone, huh?"

His voice came from right behind her head, and Lily was half ready to swear she could feel his breath on the back of her neck. Why that should give her goose bumps was something she wasn't about to explore.

"There's that keen detecting skill again," she quipped and glanced at the counter where Vickie was pouring a strawberry milkshake into a tall, frosted glass.

"I'm alone, too."

"I noticed." Lily still didn't look at him. For pity's sake. Couldn't a person get a milkshake in this town without a fuss?

"Want company?"

Vickie was on her way over and Lily took just a moment to turn around. She almost bumped her nose on his. He'd leaned in so close, he was practically draped over her shoulders. "Why do you want to sit with me?" she asked, and didn't even care if that question came out a little more bluntly than she'd planned.

"You're alone, I'm alone." He shrugged.

"Joe Biscone's alone, too." She pointed to where a huge man in a plaid shirt and faded green fishing vest sat at the end of the counter.

Ron winced. "Lily," he said, "sometimes there's a *reason* people are alone."

Her lips twitched. She didn't want to smile, but damn it, he made it tough. He was so stiff, so serious, but the look on his face when she suggested he go sit by the man who always smelled like the bass he continually caught off the dock behind his house had been priceless.

"Here you go, Ms. Cunningham." Vickie slid the pale-pink strawberry shake onto the table and then scuttled out of range as if afraid Lily was gearing up for round two.

Now it was Lily's turn to wince. "Did you see that?" she asked, and didn't wait for an answer. "That girl's going to go home tonight and tell Billy and her mother and her mother's hairdresser and the hairdresser's cousin's sister's aunt's best friend that mean old Ms. Cunningham yelled at her."

"And that's bad?" Ron asked.

"Of course it is." Lily turned back around and dipped her long-handled spoon into the whipped cream on top of the shake. Taking a bite, she licked her lips and then said, "Don't you think Mari's got enough problems lately without *me* adding to them?"

Ron eased out of his booth. Then, grabbing his hamburger and cup of coffee, he moved and sat down on the bench seat across from Lily. He watched her for a long minute and simply remembered everything she'd said.

When Lily first slid into the booth behind him, he'd

damn near groaned. All he'd wanted when he came to the Junction was a little peace and quiet. But the moment he heard that bracelet of Lily's jangling and crashing like the cymbals in a brass band, he'd known his hope was a lost cause.

Then Vickie had started in with her whispering and gossiping, and it had been all he could do to keep from turning around and chewing the girl out. But he hadn't gotten the chance. Before he could so much as open his mouth, Lily Cunningham had run to his daughter's defense. He'd smiled as her words had rushed out, fast and furious—and yet, even while he enjoyed it, he'd known that she was doing nothing more than sticking her finger in the dike.

Vickie wasn't alone in her love of gossip.

And thanks to Sheriff Bryce Collins and his insistence on treating Mari as though she were a common criminal, the whole damn town could talk of nothing else. Shamed Ron to think how much he'd always liked Bryce. How much he'd hoped at one time that Bryce and Mari would settle down together.

Just as well that hadn't happened, he told himself now. Bryce had shown his true colors. If he couldn't believe in Mari, then he damn sure hadn't loved her.

"Do sit down," Lily said, one corner of her mouth tilting into a smile that seemed to come back to haunt Ron far too often lately.

Why she was getting to him was a mystery. His

wife Violet, God rest her, had been dead ten years—
and in all that time he'd never once given another
woman a single thought. Damn it, he'd loved Violet.
She'd been everything to him.

Just keep that in mind and everything will be fine,
he told himself and grabbed for his coffee. Taking a
quick gulp, he nearly shrieked as the red-hot liquid
ate a path down his throat. But the pain at least got
his mind off Lily's smile.

"About what you said."

"I know," Lily interrupted, holding up one hand.
"I shouldn't have shot my mouth off—"

"Thanks."

Her mouth snapped shut. Her big brown eyes
blinked at him in surprise. "What?"

He set his coffee down with a clatter. "You think
it's easy?" His voice whispered across the table as
he leaned toward her. "Walking through town,
watching people watch Mari. Talking about her, whispering? Hell, these people I've known my whole life.
And all of a sudden, it's like they're strangers."

Lily reached out, grabbed his hand and gave it a
quick squeeze. The warmth of her touch slashed
through him with all the subtlety of a lightning bolt.
He pulled his hand back.

"They're just people," Lily said, shaking her head
as she took another bite of whipped-cream-topped

milkshake. "And people, in general, love to talk about someone else's troubles."

"True." He flopped back against the seat and stretched his legs out, bumping into Lily's neatly crossed ankles and then shifting guiltily away. "But this is Binghamton. I thought—"

"That because the town was named for you, your family would be gossip free?"

"Oh, hell—'scuse me—no." He shook his head and smiled at the thought. "If anything, growing up a Bingham around here was like growing up in a fish tank. Everybody wanted to be the one to catch you skipping school or toilet papering the principal's house."

"So you already know what this is," Lily said, picking up her straw and jamming it into the frothy pink ice cream.

"Sure. Human nature. The bigger they are, the more enjoyable the fall."

"Exactly. But why," Lily wondered aloud as she lifted the straw out and watched ice cream slide down and then drip into the glass, "does it seem to be that someone is actually going out of their way to make Mari look guilty?"

"You see it, too, do you?" Eager to hear someone else echo his own thoughts, Ron sat up straight again and automatically reached for his coffee.

"Of course. I'm not blind. How can you drink coffee when its so blistering hot outside?"

"I'm not outside."

"Have some shake."

"No."

"Try it."

He scowled at her. "I stopped drinking milkshakes when I was eighteen."

"Wow." Lily's eyes widened dramatically. "I didn't know you could outgrow milkshakes. Gee, what else? Sunshine? Rainbows?" She lowered her gaze to his plate. "I see that cheeseburgers are ageless."

"Oh for—"

"You should probably break it to me gently," Lily went on, scooping up another bite of ice cream, then licking her lips with a slow, thorough motion.

Ron's stomach tightened, but damned if he could look away. "Break what to you?"

"What else is off-limits." She waved her spoon in the air like a maestro with a baton. "I mean, I wouldn't want to tempt you with anything else 'unseemly.' Lemonade, for instance, would that be all right?"

This is what he got for forgetting that Lily was crazy. "You are the most annoying woman...."

"Thank you," she said. "Shake?"

"Give it here."

She slid it across the table with a victorious grin, and he avoided meeting her eyes as he dipped his spoon into the frosty glass and pulled up a sizable portion of pink ice cream. The minute he put it in his mouth, flavor exploded. Icy cold chills raced along his spine and shot back up to his brain. The taste, the smell, the feel of the ice cream melting on his tongue, unlocked memories he hadn't dusted off in years. Summer nights. Picnics.

Sweet times with Violet.

And just the thought of his late wife's name was enough to remind him that he shouldn't be sitting in the diner sharing a milkshake with Lily Cunningham. This wasn't high school. It wasn't a date.

He'd had his share of love, and now that part of his life was over.

Pushing the milkshake back across the table to her, he said, "Thanks. Better than I remembered."

It was all better than he remembered. That sizzle of attraction, the hum of electricity in the air. And because he was enjoying himself, Ron felt guilty as hell.

Chapter Three

"I don't understand," Ron said a moment later when the awkward silence over the milkshake had passed. Maybe he shouldn't say anything at all, but this had been bothering him for months. Every time he saw her, he wondered why she'd really come. And just how long she planned to stay.

"What?"

"What you're doing here."

"Eating dinner?"

"Clever. I meant *here* in Binghamton."

"Well that's blunt."

"Yep."

"You do that to annoy me, don't you?" Lily asked, tilting her head to one side as she studied him. "The one-word answers, I mean."

"Yep." Hell, why should he be the only one irritated and annoyed? And something else, his mind whispered, but he paid no attention. If he noticed that her hair shone blond in the sunlight drifting through the plate-glass window, it was simply an observation. Right?

"That's what I thought." She paused, glanced up as the waitress delivered her hamburger and said, "Thank you, Vickie, it looks great."

"Enjoy, Ms. Cunningham."

Lily sighed. "She's still worried that I'll yell at her some more. Did you see how she walked backward from the table?"

He'd noticed. And he had a feeling a lot of people walked a wide path around Lily. Any woman who could go from calm and cool to red hot and blistering in a matter of seconds was one to keep an eye on. "Could be she was treating you like a queen."

Lily laughed outright. "More likely she was afraid I'd jump at her." She shook her head and on a disgusted sigh, added, "You'd think I'd be able to control my temper better after all these years."

"Everyone's got a temper."

"Not everyone uses it."

True. Most folks played the game of being nice

while biting their tongue to keep the angry words inside. For himself, he much preferred a good flash of temper. Truth usually spilled out then, and he'd rather know exactly where he stood with a person than to have to try to guess.

He nodded at her as he watched her slather ketchup on her hamburger bun and then drizzle a river of it across still-steaming French fries. She'd never struck him as the ketchup type, Ron thought. There was more "caviar and champagne" about her than "beer and pretzels."

"I'm better than I used to be though," she said, piling tomato, onion, pickles and lettuce onto the open-faced burger before slapping the other half of the bun down on top of it all.

"Yeah?" Fascinated now, he watched as she tipped the hamburger over, took off the bottom half of the bun and used her knife to spread potato salad on the toasted surface.

"Oh yes." Unaware of his scrutiny, she kept talking while she smoothed on another layer of potato salad. "When I was younger, I'd pick up anything within reach and throw it at the closest victim when I was in the middle of a temper. I can tell you, my brothers learned to duck at an early age."

"How many?"

"How many what?" She put the other tomato on

top of the potato salad and then slapped the bun back into place at the bottom of the burger.

He shook his head. The burger was so high now, he didn't know how she'd ever be able to get a bite. "Brothers."

"Three."

"Uh-huh. Do you *always* do that?"

"What?" She held the big burger in both hands, took a huge bite, then set the burger down and, laughing, picked up her napkin and held it in front of her face while she struggled to chew.

"Pile all that stuff on your hamburger. You probably can't even taste the meat anymore."

She chewed, held up one hand and when she'd swallowed, she said, "Of course you can. And why bother having the fixings for a burger if you don't use them? It's terrific. You should try it."

"Potato salad on a hamburger?" Ron winced. "No thanks."

"You'll eat it *with* a hamburger though?"

"Sure."

"What's the difference?"

"I eat 'em separately."

"Here's a secret, Ron," she said, grinning now at his perplexed expression. "All the food you eat ends up together, anyway. There are no separate compartments in your stomach—you know, one for tomatoes, one for meat, one for potato salad."

"You're a real comedian, aren't you?"

"I don't hear you laughing."

"I'm laughing on the inside."

"And crying on the outside?" she asked. "Not very attractive."

"Do you *see* tears?" He held up both hands as if he were surrendering to a man with a gun. "Never mind. Don't bother. Don't say anything more. Your mind's on one of the weird tracks again, isn't it?"

She grinned. "Tom, Dan and Howard."

"Huh?"

"My brothers," she said, taking another, smaller bite. "You asked about them before."

Hell, Ron could hardly remember what they'd been talking about. How could anyone keep up with the way this woman's mind worked? "You just jump onto whatever conversational track feels right at the time, don't you?"

"Doesn't everyone?"

"Right. Where are they now?"

She shrugged, but he thought he caught a glimpse of something less casual sparkling in her eyes. "In Boston."

"That where you're from?"

"Nope." She picked up two French fries and swirled them through a pool of ketchup before popping them into her mouth. "I'm from Binghamton."

He smiled. Damn it, he didn't want to like her, but it was hard not to. "Before here, then."

"Originally Boston, then Los Angeles, then New York, then...*here.*"

This is exactly what bothered him, Ron thought. She'd been everywhere, lived everywhere. Why in the hell would she come to a spot-in-the-road town like Binghamton? And why would she want to stay? She'd grown up in a world of privilege and now he was supposed to believe that she was going to be happy slurping down milkshakes and building burgers at South Junction?

No way.

She wouldn't last.

And then what would Mari do?

All of his daughter's friends were backing away from her. She'd lost a lot of her big financial backers for the research lab already. And with talk spreading, chances were good she'd be losing more. His own mother had been on the phone only that morning, arguing with a banker from Lexington. But it seemed gossip traveled pretty damn well.

The word was out.

Something was going on at the clinic and Mari Bingham wasn't to be trusted.

A fresh wave of anger crested inside him, and Ron was half surprised the top of his head didn't just blow off. Hearing his daughter talked about and whispered over as if she were a criminal was enough to make his blood boil. But there was only so much a father could do.

Mari's world was crumbling around her, and for some reason she was convinced that Lily Cunningham was going to help her turn the tide. Well, Ron wasn't. Even the best PR people couldn't fight all the insidious whispers and the fears and suspicions of the very people they were trying to hose for money.

Besides, a woman society born and raised couldn't be without society for very long. One of these days, Lily'd be off, leaving Mari high and dry, and he'd have to find a way to cushion the blow for his daughter.

"Why come here?" he asked tightly, getting back to the original conversation.

"I was invited."

"Must be more to it than that."

Lily set her burger down and reached for her shake. After taking a sip, she lifted her left hand to push her hair behind her ear. That bracelet of hers chimed musically.

"I wanted a change," she said. "I wanted to live somewhere that wasn't made of concrete."

That much he could understand. Ron could no more leave the mountains permanently than he could sprout wings and fly. He had to be where the sky was huge, the trees were green and a man could walk miles in the forest without running into another soul.

But Lily Cunningham just didn't seem the kind of woman to appreciate the simpler things in life.

"You look like you don't believe me," she said, and tipped her head again, studying him through big brown eyes that looked to him like warm, milk chocolate.

"Not sure I do."

"Fortunately for me, Mari does."

"Mari's a nice girl."

"Finally. Something we can agree on."

He leaned back in his seat and watched her as she dug into her burger again. Something about her bothered him, and he really couldn't put his finger on what it was. But as she ignored him and ate her dinner, he remembered how she'd leaped to Mari's defense. How she'd read Vickie the riot act and forced the waitress to admit that Mari just wasn't the kind of woman her enemies were making her out to be.

A surge of gratitude rushed through him, swamping the mistrust that still echoed inside him. Lily had defended his child and Ron had responded by skewering her. What did that say about him?

Hell, if his mother were here, she'd give him that fish-eyed glare she used to use on him when he was a kid.

"Look," he said, giving in to the urge to make

amends, "I want you to know how much I appreciate you standing up for Mari the way you did."

Blond eyebrows lifted. "How hard was that?"

"What?"

"To be nice to me."

He frowned and reached for his own burger. Less decorated than hers, it was still tasty and sitting there getting cold. "Wasn't hard."

"Then one would think you'd be able to pull it off more often, wouldn't one?"

"One might."

Her lips twitched. "A hardheaded man."

"That's been said before."

"I'm not surprised."

He took a bite of his burger then chewed and swallowed before speaking again. "I'm not sure about you, Lily Cunningham."

She smiled and winked at him. "Good."

"Good?"

"If you were sure of me, I'd be predictable. Boring."

"Stuffy?" He prodded, reminding her of the word she'd used to describe him.

Apparently she remembered very well what she'd called him, because she looked at him now and grinned. Her brown eyes sparkled and good humor fairly shimmered in the air around her. "Oh, very few people can pull stuffy off with any degree of success.''

"And I'm one of them?"

"Yes," she said slowly, thoughtfully as she reached for her shake again. "But I see a glimmer of hope shining around you, Ron Bingham."

"Is that so?" She kept twirling the straw through the ice cream, drawing his gaze to her red polished nails and the sapphire ring on her right hand.

"Oh yes." She sucked at her straw, and Ron told himself not to notice the pucker of her full lips. For all the good it did him. "With a little bit of effort," she said, "you could be destuffied."

"Not even a word."

"It is if I say it is."

He smiled in spite of his efforts not to. "The destuffifying process sounds painful."

"It won't hurt a bit."

Ron wasn't too sure of that. He had a feeling that spending too much time with Lily could potentially be *very* painful. She made him think too much. Feel too much. Dream too much.

And for a man who'd been emotionally asleep for ten long years, waking up was not only painful…it was dangerous.

Over the weekend, Lily had had every intention of washing her car and then planting new flowers in the pots outside her front door. Well, the car was still dirty, but there were a few empty nursery pots scattered at her feet.

She sighed, tipped her head back and stretched the kinks out of her back while staring up at the cloud-covered sky. Looked as though a storm might be coming in and she found herself hoping it would happen. Not only did she enjoy the fabulous light show of electrical storms, but rain might take the edge off the humidity.

Smiling to herself, she bent down, blew her hair back out of her face and grabbed the sides of the huge, terra-cotta pot and gave it a pull.

It didn't budge.

"Oh for heaven's sake." She stood up, frowned at the damn thing, then bent over to give it another yank. Still nothing. Although she was pretty sure she'd felt something in her back yell "uncle."

"Maybe I should have put the pot on the steps *first*." She shook her head, disgusted at her own lack of foresight. "Brilliant, Lily. Really brilliant."

Purple, red and white petunias billowed over the edges of the pot and tumbled along the sides in wild profusion. They looked cheerful—and for the moment—healthy. Of course, they wouldn't look that way for long.

Lily had a black thumb.

Every plant she'd ever bought had died a horrible

death. She either underwatered or overwatered—
didn't seem to matter. She swore that when she
walked through the local nursery choosing plants, you
could almost hear the flowers shrieking, *Not me, don't
take me!*

She loved having flowers in her yard. Loved coming home to their color and scent. She simply had no
talent for it. But that had never stopped her from trying.

"Until now," she muttered, kicking the side of the
heavy pot. Her white tennis shoe didn't protect her
toe, which only served her right, she thought as she
hopped indelicately and bit down on her lip to keep
from cursing.

It was a terrible habit, and she'd tried to put a lid
on her foul language, especially since she'd moved
into this neighborhood that was absolutely crawling
with children. On that thought, she forgot about the
stubborn pot and turned around to look out at the tree-
shaded street. The Johnson twins, age seven, were
popping caps with a hammer on their curb. Lily shook
her head. Any moment now, one or both of them
would be crying and sucking on a smashed finger.
The Danville girl, at nine, was concentrating on a
fierce game of hop-scotch—who knew kids still
played that?—with her best friend. A couple of doors
down, thirteen-year-old Kevin Hanks was busily
mowing lawns for spending money.

Lily glanced at her own grass. Time to hire Kevin again before the neighbors started complaining. Honestly, moving to a house had been such a change from her loft apartment that sometimes she was just overwhelmed by it all. But bottom line—it was worth it. She loved having her own *home*. A place she could decorate or not. A place where she could practice her scandalously bad gardening skills. A place where she could sit on the front porch and listen to the sounds of children's laughter.

A tiny ache pierced her heart, and she lifted one hand to her chest as if she could somehow smooth it away. Lily sighed a little as old dreams drifted through her mind and then dissolved again. She'd always wanted a family. Children of her own. But when she'd found out that wouldn't be happening, she'd tried to make peace with it.

At first she'd thought of adoption. Then when her husband had left her, she'd let go of that thought as well. It hadn't been common at that time for single women to adopt, and after the disaster of her marriage, getting married again wasn't even a consideration. So Lily'd forgotten about her old dreams and had tried to build new ones.

Generally speaking, she'd done a hell of a job. Top of her game in the PR business, she'd had everything that most people worked their whole lives for. And she'd tossed it aside without a second thought the moment she'd had a chance to come here.

"It was a good choice," she said, speaking aloud to make sure her subconscious heard her. "No matter what, it was a good thing, moving here."

With that she turned around to face her enemy again. The overflowing pot of petunias that would, most likely, remain on the sidewalk for all eternity...or until the latest flowers died and she could empty the dirt and start over. "There's just no way I'm gonna be able to move you."

"Need some help?"

Surprise had her spinning around, and her heart had already done a weird little twist and roll before she realized the man talking to her *wasn't* Ron Bingham. That in itself was a surprise. Every time she turned around lately, that man was there. As if he were keeping a wary eye on her.

But today, she had the police strolling up her front walk. Or at least, the sheriff. Bryce Collins gave her a quiet smile, and she forced herself to return it. He seemed a nice enough man. Tall and broad-shouldered, his gray eyes were always calm and steady, as if he could reassure people with a simple glance. And maybe that worked on most people.

However, it wouldn't be working on Lily. Bryce Collins was going after Mari. Making it seem to the people of Binghamton that she was actually guilty.

And from what she'd heard, he should have known better. Mari and Bryce had been as good as engaged several years ago—until Mari had gone off to medical school.

And maybe Bryce was just nursing a grudge, but whatever his reason, it seemed ridiculous to Lily that he could suspect a woman he'd once loved.

"Was driving by. Saw you kick that pot," he was saying in a soft, amused tone. "Figured you might want a little help moving it."

Lily stared at him for a long minute. Across the street, the Johnson boys were still snapping caps, the sharp, staccato bursts of sound like an overgrown clock ticking off seconds. Kevin's lawnmower hummed in the background, and at the end of the block a car engine revved. A perfectly ordinary summer day.

Except for the fact that she had the town Sheriff offering to play landscaper.

"Shouldn't you be out arresting Mari or something?" she snapped and instantly regretted it. Antagonizing the man was not the way to win him over to the truth.

Bryce's gray eyes narrowed, full lips thinned into a grim slash across his face. A muscle in his jaw twitched.

"I'm sorry," Lily said quickly, lifting one dirt smudged hand to smooth her hair back from her face.

"I tend to say whatever I'm thinking and, believe me, that's gotten me into a lot of trouble over the years."

His expression didn't soften. "Can't imagine *why.*" Sarcasm dripped off every word, and Lily winced.

"Right. Look." She took a step forward, ignoring the ache in her toe. "You seem like a nice, intelligent, reasonable man…"

"But?"

"But—" Lily threw both hands high and let them slap down to her thighs "—I do not understand how a reasonable man could possibly suspect Mari of anything criminal."

"Ms. Cunningham, I'm—"

"Lily."

He caught himself, nodded and said, "Lily. I'm not going to discuss an ongoing investigation with you. That's police business."

"Investigation." She snorted the word. "That you should be investigating Mari at all is criminal."

He tensed and that muscle in his jaw twitched again.

"Fine," she said, "we won't talk about it. But you should be doing some serious thinking, Sheriff."

Finally, a flicker of amusement crossed his face. "Is that so?"

"Yes. You should be thinking about *who* would want to make Mari look guilty."

Amusement fled, and once again his gray eyes were steady and cool. He met her gaze for a long, silent moment before he said, "Trust me, ma'am. I'm doing a lot of thinking."

Lily watched him closely. There was more here than met the eye. Despite how it might look to the rest of the town, Lily now had the distinct impression that a large part of Bryce Collins knew damn well that Mari wasn't involved in the drug ring. His problem was, she guessed, that being sheriff, he was forced to run down every possibility.

Whether he believed it or not.

Lily nodded slowly, took a deep breath and then let it out again. "Okay, Sheriff," she said softly, "I *will* trust you."

One corner of his mouth lifted. "Thanks."

"For now," she added, just so he would know that if she thought he was barking up the wrong tree again, she'd be right there to tell him so.

He smiled and gave her a look of approval. And Lily thought that once this whole mess was behind them, she and Bryce Collins might be able to be friends.

"So," he said. "You want some help moving that pot?"

They might have their differences, but Lily was no dummy. Why turn down a big, strong man when he's offering help? "You get that pot up onto the porch—and the matching one, too—and I'll pour iced tea."

"You've got a deal." Bryce walked to the first pot and stared down at the rioting petunias. "Look real pretty, don't they?"

"Yes," Lily said on a resigned sigh. "But that's only because they don't realize just how close death is."

"Does anybody?"

"Guess not," she said, shivering as a small chill crawled along her spine. "I'll go get that tea."

Chapter Four

Ron thought he was just a little too old to be staying up all night thinking about a great pair of legs and big brown eyes.

Apparently, though, his body didn't agree.

Damn it, Lily Cunningham was making him nuts. And that wasn't an easy thing to pull off. He was known throughout Kentucky as one hardheaded son of a bitch. When it came to business, Ron wrote the book on how to be focused. How to win by wearing your opponent down. How to never surrender. Never let the other guy see you sweat.

Well, he was sweating now.

And it had nothing to do with business.

Maybe it had to do with being trapped in the damn condo he'd thought was such a great idea a year ago. Smaller than the house he'd shared with Violet—the place where they'd raised their kids and laughed and loved—the condo was supposed to be easier on him. No memories to cloud his mind. No mementos of years gone by to tug at his heart and make his soul ache.

Instead, the place bugged the hell out of him.

For the exact reason that there were no memories there. It was empty. Devoid of character, charm, *life*. It was a place to sleep and eat and escape. It wasn't his home. He'd lost his home when he'd lost Violet.

Grumbling to himself, Ron sipped his coffee and moved out through the French doors to the balcony leading off the small dining room. The trees were still dripping water from last night's storm. Drops fell in a staccato rhythm from shiny green leaves and sounded like dozens of heartbeats.

How long had it been since there'd been another heartbeat in his house, he wondered. But he didn't even have to guess. He knew exactly how long. Since Violet died ten years before.

Oh, he was no monk. He'd never been the kind of man to go for long stretches without the company of a woman. Most of his life that woman had been Violet. After she died, it had taken nearly a year for him to find the heart or the energy to seek out company. There'd been dinner dates and country weekends. But he'd never taken any of his dates to the house he'd shared with Violet. It would have seemed like a betrayal of everything they'd shared.

And once he'd moved out and sold that house— leaving behind the gardens Violet had tended with such loving care—he'd gone on as he had been. There were still dates and weekends and women. But none of them had meant enough to him to bring them into his home.

He'd never even considered it. So why, he wondered, was he imagining Lily here? He could almost see her, standing on the balcony and looking out over the forest behind the condo. If he tried hard enough, he could almost see the morning breeze lift her blond hair off the collar of the pale-green silk robe he imagined her in.

"Perfect," he muttered thickly. Now not only was she invading his dreams at night...she was stomping through his daydreams as well. Guilt stabbed at him, and he felt like a cheating husband, which he knew damn well was ridiculous.

He took a sip of the too-hot coffee and watched a pair of squirrels race across the ground and chase each other up the trunk of a gnarled pine. "Hell, even the squirrels have more of a life than I do.''

Wincing at the sound of self-pity in his voice, Ron gave a quick look around the emptiness surrounding him, as if reassuring himself there'd been no witnesses. Nope. He was safe.

He was alone.

Like always.

When the phone rang, he lurched for it like a man reaching for a lifeline. Which was just what he was doing. Talking to someone…anyone, was better than being alone with his thoughts.

''Hello?''

A voice he didn't recognize muttered in a harsh whisper, ''Your daughter should be in jail.''

Ron stiffened, and his hand fisted on the telephone receiver. Slamming his coffee cup down onto the countertop, he snarled, ''Who is this?''

A dial tone answered him.

He couldn't even tell if the caller had been male or female. The voice had been nothing more than a scrape of sound. Rubbing one hand across his face, Ron hung up the phone very carefully, because his instinct was to crush the damn thing in his hands. This was getting out of control. And there didn't seem to be a damn thing he could do about it.

Frustration bubbled to life inside him and he fought it down. He'd never been one to sit on the sidelines and watch as the world went by. And, damn it, he wouldn't start now.

Making up his mind, he headed for the bedroom to get dressed.

The clinic was quiet.

Only the receptionist sat at her desk, and she smiled at Ron as he stepped inside.

"Morning, Mr. Bingham. Here to see Mari?"

"No," he said, already headed down the hall. "Don't mind me, Heather. I can find my own way."

And he wouldn't have to explain why he was here so early in the morning to see the PR director. His footsteps were muffled on the carpeting, and he walked even more quietly as he passed his daughter's office.

He stopped at Lily's doorway. Naturally the door was open, and since she hadn't noticed him there yet, he took a moment to watch her.

She sat at her desk, head bent over a stack of papers. Strange, but he'd never really thought about her actually *working*. Stupid, he supposed, but usually when he stopped by, she wasn't in her office. She was running all over the clinic, sticking her nose into everything.

Yet bright and early on a Monday morning, here she was, diligently concentrating on...whatever. She wore a sleeveless dark-red dress with a wide collar. Draped over the back of her chair was a soft, matching sweater. Her blond hair swung down on the sides of her face and her lips worried the tip of a pen as she studied the papers in front of her. Her nose looked pink and he guessed she'd gotten some sun over the weekend. Instantly he wondered where she'd been, what she'd been doing and *who* she'd been doing it with.

Which made no sense at all. It wasn't any of his business what she did with her off hours.

His gaze locked on her mouth for a long minute, and there was a definite tug of interest. He'd thought himself long past the time when a beautiful woman could hit him so damn hard. Apparently, though, he'd been wrong. Blast it, what was it about her that had him reacting in fits and starts?

He cleared his throat and she looked up, startled. An instant later, though, that mouth of hers curved in a smile and even her eyes seemed to glow in welcome. "Well," she said softly, "look who's here."

"So you do work, huh?"

Her smile dimmed a little and her eyes narrowed a fraction. Hell, he didn't even know why he'd said that. But maybe, he thought, it was the fact that he'd been enjoying knowing that she was glad to see him. The whole, illogical, cheating-husband sensation was back. Didn't seem to matter that it was ridiculous. It was there, and he'd just have to find a way to deal with it.

"Occasionally." She set her pen down. "Is there something I can do for you?"

"Yeah." He moved into the room, a part of his mind admiring her office, as he always did. She'd taken a nondescript cubicle with one small window and turned it into a plush working space. Style. She definitely had it. "First," he said, moving to the captain's style chair opposite her desk and dropping into it, "you can forgive me for being..."

"Crabby?" she offered, obviously more than willing to help him define his ill temper.

Ron laughed shortly. "Crabby *and* stuffy. There's a combination you don't run into every day."

"Oh, you'd be surprised how often the two go together."

"And you'd know this..."

"The people I'm constantly hitting up for money are, more often than not—"

"Like me," he provided, so she wouldn't have to repeat herself.

"Like you." She nodded and smiled again. "And handing over their money...even a tax-deductible contribution to an excellent cause...tends to make those stuffy people *very* crabby."

Good humor fairly bubbled from her, even in the face of his poor manners. Ron had a feeling that Lily Cunningham was one of those perpetually cheerful people who were generally so difficult to live with. But she would always be interesting.

That thought brought him up short. Living with Lily? Who the hell had said anything about living with her? They could hardly spend fifteen minutes together without verbal shots being fired.

"So," she said, interrupting his runaway train of thought, "what brings Your Royal Crabbiness to my humble door so early in the morning?"

"PR."

"Then you came to the right place."

"Good."

"So what do you need?"

"I need to think of a way to help Mari. This is driving me insane." His hands curled over the arms of the chair and squeezed the dark wood until he wouldn't have been surprised to feel it snap off in his hands. "Some idiot called my house this morning. Said Mari should be *arrested*."

He still could hardly believe it. Arrested. Mari. Of all people. His daughter had devoted her life to taking care of people. To seeing to it that the women in Merlyn County had the best possible obstetric care. And for that, what did she get…innuendo, gossip. The very people who should have been applauding her were, instead, the first to hurl verbal stones.

"Idiots."

Ron shot Lily a look and somehow felt better to

see the unmistakable signs of temper etched on her features. Damn, it was good to have someone share your indignation. To feel connected enough to another person that their support made a difference.

He hadn't had that in ten long years.

And to find it with Lily stunned him.

"You know," she said, leaning forward and planting both elbows on her desk, "it never ceases to amaze me just how quickly a swarm of admirers can become an unruly mob."

"I don't understand how the local people could believe any of this gossip about Mari." He pushed himself to his feet, unable to sit still for another minute. Irritation again jumped into life inside him as he stalked to her window and looked out on the greenbelt that ran alongside the clinic.

Morning sunlight dappled through the leaves of the trees, tossing cooling shade on the well-trimmed grass. A slight wind brushed through the tops of the trees, sending them swaying as though they were dancing to music only they could hear. A few young mothers sat beneath the trees, watching as toddlers stumbled and crawled. A gardener knelt beside a bed of marigolds, eagerly digging out the few weeds who'd dared to raise their heads.

He braced his hands on either side of the window frame and stared through the lacy sheers ruffling in the slight breeze slipping beneath the partially opened window. "I don't understand it." He said it again, as if repeating the words echoing inside his brain would make everything clear.

Ron had lived in this place his whole life. Grown up with most of the people who were busily trying to dig the earth out from beneath his daughter's feet.

And he just didn't get it.

"Wanna punch something?"

"What?" He looked back over his shoulder at her.

She hadn't moved from behind her desk, but she'd turned so that she was facing him. Her stocking-clad legs were crossed, and one red high heel dangled from her toes as she waved her foot back and forth.

"I asked if you would like to punch someone." She smiled and tipped her head to one side. "Not that I'm volunteering for target practice, you understand."

He shook his head, more to get his fixed gaze off her shapely legs than for any other reason. "You have someone in mind?"

"Bryce Collins?" she offered cheerfully. "I saw him myself a couple of days ago and was sorely tempted to plant one on him." She curled her right hand into a fist, and Ron smiled at her fierce expression. Her hand was so damn small, a punch wouldn't have made a dent in anybody.

But he appreciated the sentiment.

"Tempting." He turned around, braced a hip on the windowsill and folded his arms across his chest.

"*Too* tempting, actually. And that's saying something. I haven't felt the need for a good fist fight in twenty years."

"Only natural," Lily said, and reached down to slip her shoe back on before uncrossing her legs and standing up. Since the moment he'd stepped into her office, Lily's heartbeat had been thundering in her ears. Something about this man got to her like no one else ever had.

Certainly couldn't be his charm, she thought wryly. The man had as many sharp angles and stiff bristles as a concrete box filled with porcupines. But for all his glowering and grumbling, there was something in his eyes. Something that made her want to reach out to him, despite all her instincts insisting that her empathy wouldn't be welcomed.

His large frame was outlined in sunlight, leaving his face in shadow. Tall and broad, he seemed to take up an awful lot of room in her very feminine office. And in the wisp of wind drifting through the window, the scent of his cologne reached her.

She nearly smiled.

Old Spice.

No trendy, ultrahip, uberexpensive cologne for Ron Bingham. She'd seen enough of him in the past few months to know that he wasn't easily impressed by the new and shiny. He was an old-fashioned kind of man. The kind who stuck by a friend through thick and thin. The kind who didn't play games and wouldn't stand for lying or cheating.

Too bad she hadn't met him years ago.

Back when she still believed in romance and happily ever after.

But years ago he'd been married to Violet, the "love of his life," according to local gossip. The townspeople still said the woman's name with a nod and a whisper of respect, though she'd been gone for ten years.

And according to that same local gossip, Ron had never been seriously involved with any woman since Violet's death. What would it have been like, she wondered, to have been loved like that? To feel a love that lasted beyond the grave? To know that no matter what happened, there was one person in the world who would always stand beside you?

Inwardly sighing, Lily wondered, too, if the late, great Violet had known how lucky she was.

"As satisfying as it must feel to hunt down the bad guy and pummel him into the dust," she said, "it wouldn't do Mari any good."

"Yeah. I know."

"The truth will come out. You know that, too, don't you?"

"Thought I did." He pushed away from the wall and straightened up.

Worry for his daughter was clearly eating at him.

Ron Bingham was the kind of man who'd always believed in the law. The system. It was in his blood, in the way he lived his life. To be questioning it all now only served to show just how worried he was.

And Lily didn't know how she could help. But she was compelled to try.

"Haven't you been telling me for months how wonderful Binghamton is?" she asked, and met his gaze when it snapped to her. "I've only been here a few months and I know that." Lily reached out and laid one hand on his arm. Even through the fabric of his sports jacket, she felt his muscles corded tight beneath her hand and a flicker of purely female approval whispered through her.

He glanced down at her hand, then lifted his gaze to hers again. When he spoke, his already deep voice dropped until it seemed to rumble along her spine. "What makes you so damn sure?"

"Because," Lily said, taking a deep breath to still the flutter of nerves rippling through the pit of her stomach, "she's innocent."

He snorted a short laugh that didn't reach his eyes. "Wouldn't have figured you for naive."

"I'm not." Heaven knew she'd had cause enough—with her love life alone—to be cynical. But she'd fought against that tendency as hard as she'd fought to keep from being too trusting...*again.*

"Good guys always win?"

"Eventually." She believed it. Karma was a powerful force in the universe, and Lily was a firm believer in just desserts.

"Yeah? How long does that take?"

"No way of knowing."

"Not good enough."

"It wouldn't be," she said with a slow shake of her head. She felt his frustration and shared it. And she'd only known Mari a short while. What must it be like for her father to have to stand by helplessly? "No. Not for you."

He stiffened and Lily reluctantly let her hand drop from his arm, severing their contact.

"What's that supposed to mean?"

Irritation spurted to life inside her. Honestly, the man was impossible to talk to without feeling the urge to shout at him. "Well, nothing insulting, so dial it down a notch, okay?"

He blinked at her. Then his frown slowly dissolved and a very *small* smile curved his mouth briefly. "Not insulting, huh?"

"No," she said, but disgusted with the eager way his porcupine quills jutted up in self-defense, she added, "but give me a minute, and I'll come up with something appropriate."

"You would, wouldn't you?"

"In a heartbeat." She shook her hair back from her face and glared at him.

He stared down at her for so long, she almost wished for a mirror so she could check and see if she'd sprouted a third eye in the middle of her forehead.

Then he spoke, and what she wanted was distance. From him.

"Who the hell *are* you, Lily Cunningham?"

The words weren't bad, but his tone held the idle curiosity of a man looking at a bug under a microscope. Lovely. "Just who you think I am."

"A rich dilettante killing a few months in a backwater town?"

She sucked in air like a drowning man. She hadn't insulted *him,* but obviously he didn't share her restraint. "*That's* what you think of me?"

"Am I wrong?"

"Only totally." Anger now swirled where irritation had blossomed, and she let the tide rise inside her. Planting both hands on his broad chest, she gave him a mighty shove that, much to her disgust, didn't budge him an inch. "You are a completely infuriating man."

"That's been said before."

"Hardly surprising, considering." Since she couldn't push him away from her, Lily whirled around and took two fast steps.

That's as far as she got.

Ron dropped one big hand on her shoulder, holding

her in place, before he slowly turned her around again to face him. "Running away?"

"I do *not* run away from *anything*." Lily wanted to yank herself free of his grasp, but since his grip felt pretty strong, she thought she'd only look like a fish, wriggling on a hook.

"Then what's your hurry?"

She put a stopper on her temper, took a long, deep breath and prayed for patience. "Tell me why I should stand here and let you insult me in my *own* office."

He looked down at her and held her gaze. Then he said softly, unexpectedly, "I don't want you to go."

Chapter Five

Everything in her went completely *still.*

The quiet room echoed with the sound of his voice and those few, unexpected words. A soft breeze carried the scent of roses and new-mown grass. The clock on the wall ticked loudly in the silence and sounded like the pulse of the room.

For one heart-stopping moment she felt like a teenager, staring up into the quarterback's steely gaze. And just as she would have been in that situation, Lily found herself totally speechless for the first time in her life.

It didn't last long.

"Ron—"

"Don't—" He shook his head, huffed out a breath. "I don't know what the hell is going on here."

"You think I do?"

"Was hoping one of us did."

"Out of luck."

His hand tightened on her shoulder, and Lily was sure she could feel the heat of his touch seeping into her bones. He was only inches away.

His gaze never left hers. Those blue-green eyes softened, then hardened, then an emotion she couldn't identify flashed across their surfaces and was gone again in the next instant.

"I don't want this." His voice was harsh, deep, and sounded as though it had scraped its way up his throat.

"Not exactly what I was looking for, either," she said, thinking, oh, that was the biggest understatement of the century.

She didn't *want* romance.

She *sucked* at romance.

Her marriage had ended with a whimper. *Hers.* Then her next attempt at love had fizzled to a close when she'd discovered that the man she was seeing had only used her to ingratiate himself with the CEO of a company he was planning to sue. And her third and so far, final, leap into the churning waters of passion had ended when her erstwhile lover had suddenly decided he was gay.

Needless to say, she'd expended enough energy and heartache trying to find the fairy tale. And now she was just too old and cranky to be bothered with it anymore. She'd been happily single and carefree for years and she liked her life just the way it was.

And even if she *were* going to be crazy enough to try her hand at love again…it wouldn't be with Ron Bingham. The father of her employer. The widower of—from everything she'd heard—the most fabulous woman on the planet. The crabby, stuffy, *bearded* man who could, it seemed, turn her crank like no one else ever had.

Oh, this could be nothing but trouble.

His hand tightened on her shoulder. Firm, yet gentle, his touch simmered through her, making her feel a lot like a slow-cooked goose, building to a boil.

"Don't want you to go," he murmured, his gaze moving over her face as if looking for a way out, a way to escape the emotions suddenly churning in the air between them. "Don't want you to stay, either."

"Well," she said gruffly, trying for and failing to find a nonchalant tone, "that sort of leaves us at an impasse."

One corner of his mouth quirked briefly. But a moment later his features were stone-cold serious again and his eyes looked nearly bleak.

"Whatever there is between us, it can't go anywhere."

"Who said I wanted it to?"

"No one. I'm just saying—"

"You're just saying *what* exactly?" Don't push it, Lily. Just turn and walk away. Break the contact between you and leave the room. Hell. *Run* from the room. This could only get more complicated.

But she couldn't run.

Wouldn't.

Which of course, made her completely crazy.

"I'm saying you're making me think things I don't want to think. Things I haven't thought about in—"

"I'm not *making* you do anything, Ron." She interrupted him cleanly, sharply. "I won't stand here and be *blamed* for something we're both feeling and we're both unwilling to—"

He pulled her close, snaked one strong arm around her waist and tipped her head back in a ferocious kiss that stole her breath and scattered her thoughts. Lily clung to him, her knees weak enough that she had to hold on to him to remain standing.

One kiss.

One kiss shouldn't have this kind of power. That single, stray thought rocketed through her brain and caromed around like a billiard ball, ricocheting wildly.

Then there was nothing. Nothing but the touch of

his lips pressed to hers. His breath puffing across her cheeks. His beard rough against her skin. Every cell in her body tingled. She felt the rush of her blood pounding through her veins and a swirl of something warm and delicious in the pit of her stomach.

Then he parted her lips with his tongue, swept inside her warmth and stole what was left of her brain.

Breathless with anticipation, excitement, Lily wrapped her arms around him and held on. His arms tightened around her middle in an almost desperately fierce hug, fusing their bodies as one.

Their tongues dipped and danced, caressed and stroked, and Lily's blood danced in her veins. Lights exploded behind her eyes and she gave herself up to a wonder she'd never expected to find. Head spinning, she leaned into him further, silently asking for more.

Then it ended.

He pulled his head back and released her all at once, and she staggered drunkenly backward a step or two before finding her balance again. Lifting one hand, she pushed her hair away from her face and then dusted her fingertips across her still-throbbing lips. Staring up at him, she struggled for air and fought the urge to crawl right back into his arms and ask for more.

"Can't do this," he muttered thickly. Shaking his head, he stared at her. A hunger so deep and raw it made her ache, shone in his eyes. "Can't."

He tore his gaze from hers and stalked from the room, leaving her where she stood.

Lily didn't turn to watch him leave.

She stood alone, silent and shell-shocked in an office that suddenly felt too empty.

Four days later Ron pulled his car into the clinic parking lot and turned off the engine. He didn't get out. Didn't even move.

He'd been avoiding this place as though they'd hung a plague sign out front. But staying away from Lily hadn't done a thing for him. Every time he closed his eyes he saw her. In his dreams he tasted her. In his weakest moments he swore he could detect her scent wafting around his empty condo.

She was surrounding him, and he wasn't at all sure what to do about it. He couldn't avoid her forever. She worked for Mari. She'd become a part of Binghamton. They would be running into each other at business, at parties. If he kept ducking her, people would begin to wonder why and that would only feed the gossip mill.

But if he went back in there and felt the same tug and pull toward her, there'd be a different kind of gossip altogether. And that he wasn't prepared for.

People in this town remembered Violet.

They remembered Vi and him as a couple.

As two halves of a whole.

If he'd had a soul mate once—could he settle for less? Should he try to find it again? No. That would be disloyal to Vi along with being damned selfish. He'd had happiness. And that kind of love didn't get handed out more than once in a lifetime.

Right?

He released his tight grip on the steering wheel and scrubbed both hands across his face. Then he smoothed his beard, looked into the rearview mirror and met his own gaze squarely. "Don't be an ass. It's not *love* you're feeling. It's something a hell of a lot simpler."

His reflected image didn't look happy about that, but then why would it? Lowering to admit that a man his age could simply be in the grip of hormones, but there it was. He wanted Lily Cunningham, *badly*.

And now that he'd had a taste of her, that need was stronger than it had been before.

Grumbling to himself, he flung the car door open and stepped out into the afternoon sunlight. A breeze ruffled his hair, and he heard the sounds of kids playing baseball. The crack of a bat sounded loudly, and shrieks and jeers from the children were almost like music. Ron reached back into the car to pull out his suit jacket. Shrugging into it, he slammed the car door shut and headed for the clinic. Best to face this head-on, tell Lily that what had happened was a *huge* mistake and hope they could move past it.

Surely, he thought, she was as eager as he was to put this behind them. That kiss had been inappropriate as hell…and too damn good. That last part hummed through his mind, then dug deep inside him, rekindling fires he'd thought had been extinguished. Scowling slightly, he paused in the parking lot and stared at the building ahead of him.

His daughter had poured everything she had into the clinic his mother had started. His family was behind this all the way. There was enough trouble at the moment without him allowing his wants and needs to cloud the situation further.

He swept his jacket back and shoved both hands into the pockets of his slacks. Rocking slightly on his heels, he told himself that all he had to do was go in, see Lily and apologize. Tell her he'd appreciate it if they could go back to the way they'd been before he'd taken their relationship to a new level.

Simple.

So why wasn't he going inside?

"Because if you see her again, you'll kiss her again," he said aloud. Disgusted with himself, Ron sighed and decided to take a walk instead. Skirting the building, he went around the side to the open field between the clinic and the research facility.

A ball game was in progress.

The field wasn't a marked baseball diamond, but kids had never needed structure to find a way to play a game. The teams were spread out in their positions and, caught up for a moment, Ron simply stood in the shade of the building and watched the pitcher wind up.

The boy hurled a beauty at home plate and the batter, a short kid in a red sweatshirt and black jeans, swung and missed, sending blond hair swinging in a wide arc.

Ron frowned, took a step forward and stopped again. That batter looked suspiciously familiar.

Another pitch.

Another swing and a miss.

The kids in the field booed and cat-called and the kids waiting their turn at bat shouted encouragement. Ron's gaze locked on the batter. Even from a distance, he knew that blond ''kid'' in the red sweatshirt was Lily.

Amazed, he watched as she stepped out of the batter box, swung the bat a couple of times, then lifted it and pointed brazenly toward left field. He smiled to himself as she approached the plate again.

What kind of woman was this?

A wild pitch soared over her head and Ron heard her laughter as it floated to him on the breeze. He leaned one shoulder against the stone wall, crossed his feet at the ankles and let his mind wander while his gaze locked on Lily.

Another pitch flew at her. She swung. A solid

smack and the ball blew high over the shortstop's head and hurtled into the valley between left field and center. Both fielders watched it go, each of them expecting the other to go after it. When they realized their mistake, both boys started running, but it was too late.

Ron's gaze flicked back to Lily just as she rounded first base and headed to second. Her blond hair flew out behind her and her legs pumped furiously as, laughing, she kept running.

He grinned, watching her and when she pulled up at third, he wanted to cheer like her teammates, who were high-fiving each other on the sidelines. Lily jumped up and down on third base and teased the third baseman by tugging his hat down over his eyes.

When the next batter slammed a single into right, Lily raced home triumphant and did a happy victory two-step all the way to the makeshift dugout.

Ron couldn't take his eyes off her. She was so different from everything he kept expecting her to be. There didn't seem to be an ounce of New England society girl in her. She kept surprising him at every turn, and maybe, he thought, that was part of her appeal. She was so different from…Vi, he admitted with a pang of guilt that seemed to stab at him.

Violet would no more have joined a kid's pickup baseball game than she would have marched naked down Main Street. Vi had always been a perfect lady.

Quiet, gentle, unassuming. She'd drifted through his life with soft sighs and kind words. They'd never argued. Never had reason to. She'd been his best friend and the only woman he'd ever loved.

And now, to be feeling something so sharp, so hungry, for a woman her complete opposite...he felt as though a part of him was trying to say that Violet hadn't been enough. But that was wrong. He'd loved his wife. Loved their years together and the quiet, contented nights they'd spent in each other's company.

"Now," he told himself in an angry mutter. Now was the time to talk to Lily. When memories of Vi were close enough that he could almost touch her. When he'd allowed himself to remember all that she'd been, all that they'd had together. When he was his strongest.

Ron started for the sidelines, walking a wide path around right field as the next batter took his place at home plate. He kept his gaze locked on the short blond in the red sweatshirt and hurried his steps until he was nearly running across the grassy field.

Laughing with the kids, Lily was bent over, brushing dirt from the legs of her jeans and tipping her head up into the dying sunlight. The silver rings at her ears caught the light and sparkled like diamonds. As he got closer, Ron heard the music in her laughter and felt his steps—and his resolve—falter slightly.

Then she straightened, turned around and saw him. He watched as her smile faded, then deliberately brightened again. She tipped her chin up like a boxer challenging her opponent and waited for him to approach.

"You play baseball?" he blurted, wondering why he hadn't just said what he'd walked over here to say.

"I play, I run, I dance." She shrugged and reached up to push both hands through her hair, scraping it back from her face.

"Instead of working?"

"Who're you, the hall monitor?" she grumbled, then turned her head to watch as the batter smashed a ball into right field. "Way to go, Kevin!" she yelled before turning back to glare up at Ron. "Seriously. Did Mari make you my parole officer without telling me?"

"No—"

"Because if she did, we're going to have to have a talk." She poked him in the chest with her index finger for emphasis. "I didn't sign on to this job thinking I'd have a baby-sitter. I'm a big girl now, you know. I haven't needed anyone looking over my shoulder for a long time and I don't intend to have it keep happening."

The fire in her eyes started a whole different kind of burning inside him. He hadn't expected it, even knowing what kind of reaction she'd had on him in the past. Every time this jolt of attraction shot through him, it caught him as unaware as it had the first time.

Damn, this woman was like no one he'd ever known.

"That's not what I was—"

She cut him off again. "You turn up at my office...then *here*...with a scowl on your face and accusation in your voice and I don't think I deserve it."

"I never said you—"

She stopped him cold one more time, and all Ron could do was stare down at her. His reasons for walking over here disappeared, and he was caught, flat-footed and mute, just watching her. There was a smudge of dirt on her nose, a spark in her eyes, and her silver earrings danced with every movement of her head.

She was...*fascinating*.

Everything about her appealed to him—and he didn't know what the hell to do about it.

"I didn't ask you for anything, did I?" Her voice was low enough that the kids just out of hearing didn't pay the slightest attention to them. "I didn't call weeping and wailing because you ran away after giving me that great, absolutely toe-curling kiss—"

He opened his mouth.

"—which, by the way, was only *half*-good."

"You just said it was toe curling."

She sniffed. "I was trying to make you feel better."

"Thanks." He smiled.

"Don't mention it. *Really*." She shook her head again, and the wind caught her hair, tumbling it in a blond mass all around her head. "I mean, it was just a kiss, Ron. No big deal. I have, believe it or not, been kissed before—all without hunting down said kisser with a shotgun and forcing him to make an honest woman of me."

"You could do it, couldn't you?"

"What?" Her brows lowered, her eyes narrowed and she tilted her head to one side.

"Hunt a man down."

"If I had to."

"You'd never have to," he murmured, not really sure he'd actually said the words aloud until he saw the surprise flicker in her eyes. Then he blew out a breath, caught her elbow in a firm grip and drew her farther away from the kids clustered near them.

"What's going on, Ron?" She pulled her arm free and looked up at him.

Ron rubbed the tips of his fingers together as if he could still feel her within his grasp. Then a moment later, stuffed his empty hand into his pants pocket. "I came over here to tell you that kiss was a mistake."

"Fine." She backed up. "I *had* already figured that out—but now you've told me."

"Do you never shut up?"

"Almost never."

"Try it now."

"Why should I?"

"Because I asked you to, damn it." That came out a little gruffer than he'd planned, but it was too late to call it back. Good thing, too, since she nodded abruptly, folded her arms across her chest and dramatically closed her lips tight.

Now that he had the floor, so to speak, he wasn't at all sure what he should say. Oh, he knew what he wanted to say. And he knew what common sense insisted he say. Instead, he went another way entirely.

"I want to kiss you again."

"Huh?"

"You said you'd shut up."

"Right." Those lips folded on top of each other again, but her eyes were speaking volumes.

"Maybe it was a mistake. Probably. Okay, yeah, it was." He pushed one hand through his hair, then reached out for her before letting his hand fall to his side again. "Doesn't seem to matter. I want you. And I'm not sure what I'm gonna do about that."

She snorted a laugh, silence forgotten. "Don't you think I'll have a little something to say about that."

"Nope."

Blond eyebrows lifted. "Really."

"Lily," he said, taking a step closer until all that

separated them was the fabric of their clothing, "if I want you, I'll *have* you."

She sucked in a small gasp of air and swallowed heavily. "Think pretty highly of yourself, don't you?"

A sharp, cold breeze kicked up, lifting her hair and carrying her scent to him until Ron could have sworn he was drowning in it. He closed his eyes, opened them again and looked down at her.

"Thinking pretty highly of that kiss."

"And?" she said on a whisper.

"And—" he lifted one hand to touch her cheek "—I'm thinking we'd only get better with practice."

Chapter Six

Hey, Ms. Cunningham!''

Lily turned her head and looked at her neighbor boy, Kevin Hanks, standing in the infield, shielding his eyes with the flat of his hand. The boy's jeans were ripped out at the knees and his T-shirt was covered with dirt and grass stains. "Yes?"

"We're callin' the game on account of Mike's gotta get home, and it's his ball."

Lily laughed shortly. How much simpler life was when you were a child. The rules were clearly defined. The world made sense. And nothing was more complicated than finding another ball.

''All right, then,'' she called back. ''Be careful going home.''

''Yes ma'am,'' Kevin answered, already turning to sprint and catch up to his friends.

''And don't forget about my lawn,'' Lily yelled after him, since Kevin had promised to mow it the next day, and she didn't want him forgetting. Much longer and her front yard would qualify as a meadow.

He waved one hand in the air to show her he'd heard, but he didn't look back.

Then she was alone with the man who'd been avoiding her for days. Strange, she'd gone over this very meeting in her mind dozens of times. She'd imagined it happening in a hundred different ways. She'd pictured him bumping into her at the clinic— or even stopping by her house. She'd thought of any number of pithy, brilliant, even cutting, remarks she could make when the opportunity presented itself.

But now that she was faced with the situation she'd been expecting, she felt almost at a loss. Because it wasn't going at all the way she'd assumed it would.

Oh, Ron was still crabby and irritating as only he could be. But he was also saying things she wasn't sure how to respond to. And now that the boys were gone and they were alone again, Lily had no idea what was coming next.

So naturally, she went on the offensive. Simply put,

it was the best way she knew to defend herself—and her heart.

"Let me get this straight," she blurted, when she turned around and looked up at him again. "You came here to tell me that the kiss was a mistake, but you think we'd do better with practice."

"Essentially."

She frowned at him. "That makes no sense at all."

"Sure it does."

"In which universe?" Good. Irritation was much better than attraction. Safer. Cleaner. Less complicated.

He reached for her, but Lily took a quick step back, keeping out of his reach. It would be much easier to keep her defenses up if he wasn't touching her.

Ron blew out an exasperated breath, but nodded. "Okay. We'll do this your way."

"This is *not* my way."

"Right. Anyway," he went on quickly, to keep her from speaking again. "The kiss was great. A mistake, but great. And even though repeating it would be a bigger mistake, I've no doubt it would be even better the second time."

Lily's head swam with new images. His mouth on hers. His hands sweeping up and down her spine. His broad, muscular chest pressed against her. Her blood spurted and danced in her veins, made her brain fuzzy and the edges of her vision swim.

She pushed those thoughts aside, though, and forced herself to pay attention to the moment at hand.

"Even if it would, you're not interested, remember?" she said tightly.

"That's the problem," he admitted, shoving both hands through his hair in a gesture of frustration. "I *am* interested."

That little dance of anticipation and eagerness swept through her again. It seemed logic and common sense had little to do with what her body was feeling. What her *heart* wanted to believe.

Long minutes ticked past with neither of them speaking. Neither of them broaching the silence that hung between them as heavily as the humid, afternoon air. Another stray, cool breeze drifted past, ruffled Lily's hair, then moved along, disappearing into the trees lining the back of the clinic.

Ron stared off into the distance, as if looking for answers he couldn't find. But at last he turned his gaze back to Lily and stared into her eyes with the same searching strength as before and said, "I loved my wife."

Lily blinked up at him. Whatever she'd been expecting to hear from him, it hadn't been *that*. "Of course you did."

He spoke again as if she hadn't said anything at all. "I never cheated on her in all the years we were together."

"Good for you."

"Never even considered it."

Confused now, Lily just looked at him. But damned if that flicker of irritation didn't jump into life again at the pit of her stomach. "And do you want a medal for that?" she asked, feeling almost as though she were defending the long-dead Violet's right to expect a faithful husband. "Recognition somehow for doing what you were *supposed* to do?"

He scowled at her as if he'd bitten into something distasteful and didn't know where to spit it out. "No, damn it."

"Then what's this about?"

He stalked away a few paces, then turned around and stomped right back again. "It's about that this is new to me. All of it."

"Huh?"

"Finally put a stopper on that whole clever thing, didn't I?" His words were pleased, but his expression still read "frustrated."

"Just say what you're trying to say, already."

"That's part of it, damn it. I don't know how to say it, any more than I know how to feel it."

"If you're trying to confuse me, you're doing an excellent job."

"There's something here, Lily. Between us. Something I'm not sure I'm interested in, but something that's big enough I can't ignore it."

Her heart skittered, and her throat nearly closed. Nothing like hearing that a man was interested in you against his better judgment to make a woman feel *special.* "I don't know what I'm supposed to say to that."

"Believe it or not," he nearly snarled, "I'm not looking for your opinion."

"Good to know, thanks." That said it all, she guessed. He was apparently twisting in his own wind of indecision, and she was merely a spectator. "So basically, you're just interested in my mouth—not what comes out of it."

"If you were easier to talk to…"

"Excuse me?" Lily interrupted him with surgical precision. "This is somehow my fault? I was minding my own business playing baseball and *you're* the one who came over with a confessional attitude, looking for absolution."

"I didn't say that—"

"Of course you did." She lifted one hand to push her windblown hair back from her face and only vaguely heard the tinkling music from her platinum charm bracelet. "You're attracted to me, but you don't want to be. You're a faithful husband, but your wife's been gone ten years."

"Just a minute—"

"And," she held up one hand and kept talking. "You'd like me to know that you liked kissing me,

but you won't be doing it again even though it might get better— No." She caught herself. "Wait a minute." She studied him as though he were a tablet engraved with hieroglyphics and she wasn't quite sure of the translation. "You won't be kissing me again *because* it might get better."

He inhaled sharply, deeply and looked around the empty field as if searching for help that wasn't there. Then his gaze snapped back to hers—almost guiltily. "Maybe. Maybe that's it."

Lily shook her head. "You're a piece of work, you know that?"

He blew right past that. "You confuse the hell out of me, and I'm not used to that."

"Well, to coin a phrase...*duh*."

He smiled briefly and snorted out a choked laugh. "See? That. I'm not used to dealing with a woman like you."

"Like *me*." Lily folded her arms across her chest, more for the comfort of a solitary hug than anything else. "You've said that before. Define it."

"Easier said than done."

"Try."

He looked out over the empty field where only moments before children had been playing, yelling, laughing. The afternoon was quickly sliding toward twilight. A few birds chattered at them from the trees.

From the parking lot came the sound of an engine revving in place. "You were playing *baseball*."

She frowned. "So?"

"So. Most women your age—"

"Hey!"

"Sorry. Most *grown women* wouldn't be running around in a field playing baseball with a bunch of kids."

"That's a shame, if you ask me," Lily said tightly. Here it was. All her life people had looked at her warily. She'd never believed in coloring between the lines. She'd always preferred a scribbled picture to one that was rigidly accurate. So she marched to a different drummer. Did that really have to qualify as a capital offense?

Here in Kentucky, she'd found people to be more accepting. If she started singing along with the recorded music in the grocery store, more often than not, one of her fellow shoppers would join in, trying for a badly done harmony. If she wanted to wear black jeans and tennis shoes to work one afternoon, and then spontaneously join a baseball game, her co-workers thought nothing of it.

So *why* she asked herself, did she have to be attracted to the *one* man who *did* care? Why did it have to be stuffy Ron Bingham that had her staying awake nights, thinking of long, slow kisses and soft sweet caresses? Why hadn't she learned enough to train her heart to be more picky?

"Maybe it is."

"Of course it's a shame," she snapped. "Why should we forget to have a good time because we're not kids anymore?" She took a step toward him and was pleased when he took a step back. "Why should we worry about dancing in the kitchen if there's no one to see? Why does it make more sense to guard our every emotion and thought and action than it does to just simply relax and enjoy life? Why does everything have to be a major decision?"

"I didn't say it did."

"You kissed me," she said, moving another step closer. "I kissed you back. Big deal. The world didn't explode. Your children didn't turn their backs on you. The loyal villagers didn't storm 'Bingham Castle' with flaming torches."

Another short, choked-off laugh shot from his throat, and he looked as surprised by it as she was. Okay, she was going way over the top here, even Lily knew it. But she wasn't going to stand there and let him make a federal case out of nothing.

"It was a *kiss* for pity's sake. And if it gives you *this* much trouble, then God help you. Because your life really needs shaking up."

"I suppose it does."

"Oh, trust me on this one," she said. "It *really*

does. You're so locked up and closed off you wouldn't know a good time if it came up and bit you on the ass.''

He blinked and laughed again. One corner of his mouth lifted and even with the stupid beard, she could see that the crooked smile stayed this time. It didn't retreat.

''You're right,'' he admitted after a long minute of Lily trying to catch her breath and come up with yet another string of entertaining insults.

And his simple agreement threw her off.

''What?''

''I said you're right.'' He stepped in closer, eliminating the slight space that had separated them. Lily felt as though he'd taken more than a physical step. It was as if he'd crossed some unseen boundary that had been keeping him at an emotional distance.

And she wondered if she ought to be glad of it—or worried.

Lily thought about moving away again, but damned if she'd step back. Now that he was moving forward, was it any time for her to put it in reverse? ''Well, that's certainly a good way to end an argument—surrender.''

''When I'm outgunned and outflanked?'' A dry chuckle rolled from his throat as he smiled. ''Hell yes, I'll run up the white flag.''

''I should have attacked sooner,'' she muttered.

"You have been," he pointed out. "I've just been dodging the salvos aimed at my head."

"Pretty nimbly, too, I might add."

"Thanks," he said wryly.

"Oh, no problem." She held up one hand. "No, wait. Let me rephrase…"

His smile broadened, and there was something in his eyes that shouted at her. Something warm and welcoming and, heck, probably dangerous. But she was in the middle of things now, and Lily was no quitter. So she stood her ground and waited for whatever was going to come next.

"I have been closed off." Ron reached for her, dropping both hands to her shoulders and holding on, as if half expecting her to bolt for the tree line. "For more years than I'd care to think about, I've been going through the motions."

"Why?"

"Not important right now."

Yes it was, she thought, warning bells clanging in her head even while her blood rushed and her heart lifted. His hands on her shoulders sent spears of heat and light to all of the dark, empty corners of her heart. And she didn't want that light. Not now. Not this way.

Because she knew that the light wouldn't be staying.

The heat would go away again.

Oh, she so didn't want to set herself up for another fall. And with that thought in mind, she should have pulled away from him. Turned her back and headed for the clinic. Where there were patients and nurses and midwives and noise. Enough distractions to keep either of them from feeling what they were feeling and thinking what they were thinking.

But she couldn't walk away.

Not while his hands were on her.

Not while his gaze was locked with hers.

A part of her brain shouted out the fact that they were in plain view of whoever might happen to glance out the clinic windows. But a louder, more needy voice called out, *Who cares?*

"Meeting you, though," he said, his gaze now shifting, sliding over her features like a whispered touch, "has changed a lot in my life."

"Uh-huh." It was the best she could manage.

"You make me feel things I'd thought were gone from my life. You make me *want* things I haven't wanted in a long time."

"And that's bad?"

"That's…where the confusion comes in."

Lily knew damn well she'd regret this. Heck, a part of her *already* regretted it. If something happened between them and then sputtered out of existence, she'd be stuck here, living in a tiny town where everyone would know about her latest heartache. She couldn't be sure, but it might even affect her job. What if Mari took exception to the woman who toyed with her father's affections? What if beginning something with Ron, ended something in her new life?

There were too many what-ifs.

Too many pitfalls looming in front of her to even be considering this.

But she heard herself say the words, anyway. And she knew she meant them. "This...what's between us...it doesn't have to be anything more than what it is."

His hands tightened on her shoulders, and his eyes darkened until they were the color of a stormy sea. "I'm too old for stolen kisses and sneaking around."

"Who said anything about sneaking?" Lily countered. "We're both adults. Both single—"

He winced but she plowed right ahead.

"Why shouldn't we—"

"Have an affair?" he finished the thought for her.

"Well that sounds a little tacky...you know, drive-bys at a motel on the outskirts of town."

He snorted. "Wouldn't want to be tacky."

"No reason for it."

"Don't suppose there is," he said, and bent his head closer, closer.

She felt his breath on her face. Felt the heat rising from his body and reaching out to hers. Felt herself bend, her body moving toward his, her face tipping up, her lips parting in anticipation.

"An affair?" he whispered.

"Sound exciting?" she asked.

He stopped, stared at her hard for a long minute. Lily would have given anything to know what was wheeling through his brain at that moment. But his emotions were shielded behind a swirl of desire clouding his eyes.

And for that one moment, the desire—for her—was enough.

"I was never an 'affair' kind of guy."

She knew that, just by knowing the kind of man he was. And still she said, "Times change."

"Yeah, they do."

"So." She swallowed hard and risked her heart with a simple question. "You interested?"

A long pause cost her an agony of uncertainty until he answered, "Oh, yeah."

His mouth moved closer still. Just a breath away now. Lily held her breath and tried to hear past the rush of her own blood and the thundering of her own heartbeat.

Then their lips met and a rush of sweet longing pushed through her body, making her grateful for the support of his broad, muscular chest. His hands dropped from her shoulders to her waist and as he wrapped his arms around her, Lily surrendered herself to the sensations rattling through her.

Desire gripped her by the throat and squeezed.

Every inch of her body pulsed with a driving, primitive need that she'd never known before. Not even when she was a kid and in the first throes of passion. What she'd experienced then had been fumbling, grappling youth. Exploration, discovery.

This was different.

Exploration was different now.

The territory was familiar, achingly so, but the journey to the heart of it was unique. Marked by galloping heart rates and strangled breath.

He touched her; she moved into him.

She sighed; he groaned.

His tongue caressed; hers responded.

He swallowed her breath and gave her his.

A soft warm wind wrapped itself around them, entwining them in the scents of summer. As if from a distance, the sound of that same wind dancing through the leaves of the nearby trees sounded like a symphony of sighs.

Lily's arms wound around Ron's waist and held on for dear life. All around her, her world was shattering. Tipping on its axis.

But she couldn't seem to care.

All she wanted, all she could think about was the next kiss. The next touch. The next sigh.

She wanted to feel his hands on her naked skin. She wanted to lie alongside him in the moonlight and define every hard-muscled inch of him with her fingertips. Images filled her mind and left her shaken. She'd never known such an incredible sense of need. It spiked higher and faster than she'd ever experienced before.

Lights exploded in her brain, dissolving any further attempts at rational thought. She didn't mind a bit. There would be time later for rehashing this. For rethinking it and wondering if she'd done the right thing, said the right thing.

If it had been as magical for him as it was for her.

His mouth slid from hers, down along her jaw and to her neck. Lily tipped her head back and stared at the cloud-streaked sky leaning toward twilight. His mouth moved over her skin, his tongue traced warm, silky patterns across her neck, and she shivered as the sky above her darkened into a soft, violet haze.

"Lily," he murmured, and his voice seemed to vibrate inside her. He lifted his head and stared down at her.

She blinked to clear her hazy vision and met his eyes, stormier now, darker and yet wilder.

"I don't know where this is going," he said thickly, as if every word had been squeezed from a too-tight throat. "All I know is, I want you."

Lily sighed and reached up to cup his face between her palms. "Good."

Chapter Seven

Blood rushed back into Ron's head. His vision swam for a split second before clearing and focusing in on the woman in front of him.

Lily Cunningham.

The woman making him crazy.

Her brown eyes sparkled, the flash of silver at her ears winked in the dying light of the sun, and her mouth—that incredible mouth of hers—smiled and tempted him into another taste.

He didn't take it.

Because he knew if he had one more taste he'd need another and then another. Considering that they were standing in the middle of an open field, and easy prey for anyone with a tendency for snooping, that probably wasn't a good idea.

Besides, saying he was ready for an affair was easier than actually beginning one. The word *affair,* at least to him, brought up mental images of sneaking around, cheating on your spouse, avoiding private detectives. Stupid. Hell, he knew it was stupid. Vi had been gone a long time, and it wasn't as if he'd lived like a monk for the past ten years.

But this was different.

Lily was different.

She wasn't the kind of woman he could take out to dinner and then casually forget about.

Time spent with Lily would be etched into his mind. He knew that already. For the simple reason that he lay awake every night, remembering every moment he'd spent with her. The way she smiled. The way she laughed.

God help him, the *taste* of her.

He'd known from the moment he first saw Lily that she was going to shake up his life. The only question remaining was…did he *want* his life to be shaken?

"Looking for a way out?" she asked, and doubt shimmered in her big brown eyes.

"No," he said, quickly enough to convince her and disguise his own doubts. "Just thinking I'd like to take you to dinner."

She blinked up at him, clearly surprised. Pure Lily, he thought wryly. She could blithely suggest an affair and then be jolted by the idea of a dinner invitation.

"You mean a *date?*"

"Is that so hard to imagine?"

"No. I just didn't expect it," she said, staring up at him as if trying to divine his thoughts. Good luck with that. Hell, even *he* couldn't make sense of his thoughts.

"Good. About time *I* did something unexpected, don't you think?"

She tilted her head to one side and studied him through thoughtful eyes. "The de-stuffifying process?"

"Not as painful as I might have thought."

"Glad to hear it."

She smiled, and Ron's gaze fixed briefly on her mouth. It took a second or two to force himself to meet her gaze again. "I can pick you up in an hour?"

Lily checked the delicate platinum watch on her left wrist. "An hour?" Then she glanced down at herself, noticing as if for the first time her dusty jeans, battered red tennis shoes and the grass stain across the front of her sweatshirt. Wincing, she looked up at him again. "Can we make that *two* hours?"

Ron laughed and took her elbow, turning her toward the clinic and the parking lot beyond. "Fine.

Two hours. Then I'll take you to a dinner that'll knock your socks off."

"I won't be wearing socks."

"You'll like it anyway."

"Which restaurant?"

"You'll find out."

"It's not a cook-it-yourself kind of place is it?" she asked on a short laugh. "Because if it is, I think I should warn you that the fire department in New York actually *banned* me from cooking of any kind when I—"

She stopped dead when a police car, lights flashing, siren wailing, pulled into the clinic parking lot and stopped with a screech just outside the doors. Even from a distance, they both recognized Bryce Collins as he jumped from the car and slammed the door behind him. The tall, dark sheriff then walked toward the clinic like a man on a mission.

"What on earth?" Lily muttered.

"Hell. What *now?*" Ron countered, already hurrying his stride, pulling Lily along in his wake.

By the time they pushed through the door, the waiting room was in chaos. A handful of patients were chattering, shouting questions, then answering themselves when no real information came their way. A two-year-old boy, startled by all the activity, sat at the children's table, mouth open in a howl of displeasure while tears tracked along his fat cheeks. A teenage girl, obviously in labor, sat in a corner, huffing and blowing, while keeping her interested gaze fixed on the commotion.

Heather, the receptionist, had planted herself in the middle of the hallway and was glaring up at Bryce as he tried to push past her.

"Damn it, it's my job," the sheriff said tightly.

"Your job sucks, Bryce." Heather planted both small hands on his chest and gave him a shove. He didn't budge, which only made her try harder. "Now, you get out of here and let us get on with business."

"I'm *here* on business," Bryce told her, raising his voice to be heard above the uproar. "And if you don't get out of my way, I'll arrest you for getting in the way of that business."

"You arrest me, Bryce Collins," Heather snapped back, "and I will make your life a living hell. You can't go around arresting law-abiding citizens."

"If you're obstructing justice, you're not law abiding, are ya?" He snarled the question, sending a searching gaze over the top of her head and down the hall.

The toddler cranked it up a notch, and Ron winced as he made his way through the crowd to get closer to Bryce and Heather. Lily scooped up the crying child and dropped him onto her hip, jiggling him sympathetically while following Ron through the cluster of pregnant women.

"What's going on here?" Ron demanded. His voice, the deep, rolling sound of authority, cut through the noise and demanded silence.

Lily worked her jaw in the sudden silence, as if trying to unpop her ears, but then the child on her hip snuffled loudly and she knew her hearing wasn't damaged. It was just Ron's natural ability at leadership that had reestablished order.

Bryce turned his head and looked at Ron. Fury and frustration simmered in the sheriff's dark eyes, and Lily's heart dropped. She felt it sink lower in her chest and knew that whatever was happening was about to get worse.

"I've got to see Mari," Bryce muttered, shooting another steely glare at Heather, who hadn't moved an inch. *"Now."*

Heather sniffed and folded her arms across her chest, silently daring him to try to get past her.

Ron leaned in and took hold of Bryce's upper arm. "What's going on here and why are you creating such havoc in this place?"

"Damn it, Ron," Bryce said in a furious whisper, "this is official business. I don't have to talk to you. My business is with Mari."

"She's busy," Heather snapped. "Like I told you already."

"Tell her to get unbusy."

She snorted and gave him an up and down look that told him in no uncertain terms she thought he was the biggest jackass she'd seen in a long time. "Uh-huh. Let me just run back to room five and tell Loretta Sanchez to cross her legs and go into unlabor."

Bryce snatched at his hair with both hands. "There has to be someone else here to deliver that baby."

"Loretta's Mari's patient and you know she won't leave when she's needed."

"No," he grumbled. "She wouldn't. Not now."

"Bryce..." Ron spoke up again and Lily sidled close enough to listen in.

She wasn't proud.

Eavesdropping worked.

That's why so many people did it.

"I can't talk about this with you, Ron," the sheriff said, finally glancing around at the audience watching him as if noticing them for the first time. His gaze slid away from the interested women gathered in close and focused on Ron again. "It's important I talk to Mari."

Lily's heartbeat skittered unsteadily, and she wrapped her left arm around the toddler on her hip, seeking as much consolation as she was giving. Something was terribly wrong here and these two men weren't going to find a way through it without some help.

"All right everyone," she called out into the uneasy quiet. "Why don't you all sit down? Heather will make some coffee—" she looked at the tear-stained face of the boy on her hip, and Lily's heart rolled. He was beautiful. Big brown eyes, soft, blond-ish-brown hair and a chocolate mustache that he'd already transferred to her sweatshirt. "And I'll bet Heather can even find you another cookie," she said. "Would you like that?"

He brightened instantly and threw both hands high as if he was doing a personal, one-baby wave. "Cookie!" he crowed and every woman in the place chuckled, which was enough to ease the tension layering the room.

"'Atta boy," Lily murmured, and stepped between Bryce and Heather as if unaware of the fury simmering between them. Handing the child off to the receptionist, Lily jerked her head toward the waiting room and said, "Take care of everyone in there, all right? I think Tina, over in the corner, there, is pretty serious about labor this time."

"She was last week, too," Heather said with a tired sigh. "I *told* her to stop eating burritos at dinner. Gives her gas, and she screams 'labor.'"

Lily ignored Ron and Bryce and focused on the tiny woman in front of her. "Well, this might be the real thing. So you take care of things out here, and I'll take care of these two. Deal?''

Heather's sharp gaze swept from Ron to Bryce and back to Lily. "You got the worst end of that deal."

"Wouldn't be the first time," Lily said with a chuckle that sounded as forced as the smile she'd plastered on her face. But she made that smile brighter as she turned and looked up at the two men watching her. "As for you two—in my office."

"Lily—" Ron started.

"Ms. Lily—" Bryce spoke up at the same time.

She held up one finger like an elementary school teacher warning her charges. "No more. Not out here. Not one more word. *Either* of you."

With that, she spun around and marched down the long hall toward her office, never stopping to see if they were following her. She knew they would be. What choice did they have? They couldn't see Mari at the moment, and they wouldn't have any luck dealing with Heather. So Lily was all they had left.

She walked into the room and instantly felt more in charge. Whatever had happened, they would handle it. Whatever Mari needed, Lily, personally, would see to. Nothing could be as bad as what had been running through her mind out in the waiting room. That, ridiculously, Bryce had come to *arrest* Mari Bingham.

The very idea was absurd.

Wouldn't happen.

At least, not if Lily had anything to say about it.

The two men took the turn and tried to enter the office at the same time. Two pairs of broad shoulders weren't going to fit, and Lily sputtered at the men, neither of them willing to be the one to back away.

"For heaven's sake," she snapped, and grabbed hold of Ron's coat sleeve. She tugged him forward, Bryce followed directly after, and then, for the first time since she had come to work at the clinic, she shut her door.

"Ms. Lily," Bryce started to say.

"*Just* Lily," she said, interrupting him quickly. "*Ms.* Lily makes me sound like a saloon dancer."

Ron smirked, and she shot him a look. Just minutes ago, she'd been wrapped in his arms and lost in his kiss. Now she wanted to kick him. "As for you, you weren't helping the situation out there, you know."

Bryce's eyebrows lifted, and he pursed his lips as if about to whistle innocently. Ron stared at Lily. "I was *trying* to help."

"By shouting in that lord-of-the-manor tone?" She shook her head. "Not helping." Then she turned on Bryce. "And you should know better than to storm into a place of business—a business where women are in pain and needing comfort and solace—and start throwing your weight around as if you're the FBI or something."

Ron smiled as Bryce got his share of Lily's tirade,

but a quick look from her wiped that smile off his face.

"Lily," Bryce said tightly. "I'm the sheriff. *I* decide what's right. And which way I do my job."

She wasn't impressed. Lily took a step closer and tipped her head back so she'd have no trouble meeting his gaze directly. "And you decided to cause a riot? Was that the best you could come up with?"

"There was no riot."

"Damn close," Ron muttered.

"If you need to see Mari, then you can wait until it's convenient," Lily said, ignoring Ron's comment.

"Convenient?" Bryce echoed, clearly astonished. "You think I wanted to be here? You think I *like* accusing a woman I once—" He caught himself before he could bring up the subject of love. "I didn't *want* to see her today. I *have* to see her."

The underlying tone of pain in his voice suddenly reached both Lily and Ron. Worry shone in Bryce's eyes and his body nearly vibrated with tension. Lily's gaze snapped to Ron's, and he instantly moved closer to Bryce.

Lowering his voice, he asked, "What's going on? What do you need to see Mari about?"

Bryce shook his head. "Can't tell you that. It's police business, Ron."

The older man stiffened slightly. "I've known you

since you were a kid, Bryce. Our families go to the same church."

Bryce nodded, but he didn't look happy about it.

Lily braced herself.

"Mari's my daughter," Ron said. "You know damn well I'll be standing right beside her when you finally tell her, so save some time and spill it now."

Bryce's gaze shot to Lily, and she suddenly felt exactly what she was.

The outsider.

Regret crowded her chest, but she lifted her chin and said softly, "I'll be outside. Use the office as long as you need."

She reached for the doorknob, but Ron's voice stopped her. "Don't go."

Lily glanced over her shoulder at him. His gaze locked with hers. "Stay. You're…a friend. Mari might need one."

She nodded and came back into the room, taking up a spot just beside Ron. Silence blossomed and grew in the room until it was a living breathing thing that clawed at the air.

Finally, when even *he* couldn't stand it any longer, Bryce spoke up. "Fine." Looking at Ron, he ignored Lily and said, "We just raided a house. Nabbed two suspected drug dealers."

A shiver of warning trickled along Lily's spine, and she just managed to keep from shuddering. Drugs.

Again. The Orcadol? For months now, the clinic—and Mari in particular—had been under suspicion of selling Orcadol, a powerful pain medication, on the black market. Naturally, there was no basis at all to the ridiculous claims. But Mari's life had been in turmoil, and a cloud of mistrust had been hanging over the clinic and everyone working there for far too long.

They certainly didn't need yet another round of accusations and innuendo.

As she fought to maintain a stoic air of nonchalance, a headache of monstrous proportions leaped into life behind her eyes. The throbbing pounded in time with her own heartbeat, and she wondered why her head didn't just simply explode.

"What's that got to do with Mari?" Ron demanded, taking a step toward the younger man as if wanting to grab him and give him a good shake.

Bryce's jaw clenched, his features screwed into a mask of distaste, and he reached up to unbutton the top left pocket of his uniform shirt. Then from that pocket he pulled a plastic bag with a few papers sealed inside it.

Worried now, Lily swallowed hard and tried to ignore the pain in her head and the sinking sensation at the pit of her stomach. As Bryce handed the bag to Ron, Lily stepped close enough to look at the papers.

"What's this?" Ron demanded without even looking at them.

''Oh, God.'' The soft exclamation slid from Lily's lips before she could stop it.

''Yeah.'' That one word left Bryce on a resigned sigh before he told Ron, ''We found these prescription papers—more than half a dozen—hidden in one of the perp's bedroom. Stuffed between the mattress and the boxspring.''

''So?'' Ron's fingers tightened on the bag, but still, he refused to look at the evidence Bryce had handed him.

''We can't make out the name of the prescribed drug,'' Bryce said. ''But the doctor's signature is clear enough. It's Mari's. And the suspect is not one of her patients.''

The room tilted.

But that couldn't be.

Lily shook her head to find her balance again and looked from Mari's scrawled signature up into the bleak eyes of the young woman's father. A slow count of three passed before she saw refusal and denial lift up in Ron's hazel eyes.

''No way,'' he ground out, shoving the incriminating evidence back at Bryce as though touching it had contaminated him.

''Damn it, Ron, it's right there. Plain as day.''

Ron barked out a sharp, almost painful-sounding laugh. ''Bryce, you could show me a picture of my daughter standing on a street corner, passing out drugs to kids and I still wouldn't believe it. There's something else going on here. Mari doesn't deal drugs. And you *know* it. Damn it, you know *her*."

"I used to," Bryce said. "A long time ago."

"Then remember it," Lily said, speaking up for the first time. She grabbed Ron's hand and was pleased to feel him squeeze her fingers, hard. "Remember the woman you knew. The woman you *loved*. Mari Bingham is one of the finest women I've ever known. And I believe you know that, too."

Bryce's gaze fixed on her for a long minute, and Lily saw the pain and disbelief shining in his eyes. But she also saw determination and that worried her. Bryce Collins was a man as devoted to his work and to the preservation of the law as Mari was to her profession. He would do what he had to do, no matter what it cost him.

When he spoke a moment later, he confirmed her thoughts.

"Doesn't matter what I believe," Bryce said, his voice a low rumble of sound in the otherwise still room. "Only matters what the evidence says. And this evidence says Mari's got some explaining to do."

As if appearing on cue, there was a knock on the door and then Mari stepped in, a wide smile still on her face. "Loretta had a boy. Eight pounds, ten ounces and the proud father is already signing him up for football!" She stepped into the room, let her gaze sweep across the faces of the people gathered there and slowly her smile faded away. "What is it? Dad? Bryce?"

Lily held onto Ron's hand as Bryce faced Mari with the prescription papers. She watched, silently, as the young woman she loved so dearly, stared in disbelief at her own signature on the damning evidence.

"This is impossible," she whispered, shaking her head for emphasis. "I mean—it sort of looks like my writing, but it's not."

"Mari," Bryce said softly. "I need you to come to the station with me."

Ron stepped forward, and Bryce stopped him with one upraised hand. "Just to talk," he said.

"I'll call our lawyers," Ron told him.

"That's your prerogative."

Mari's gaze lifted to the man she'd once loved beyond all measure. "Are you saying you think I need a lawyer?"

"I think you should be safe."

"Do you believe I'm involved in this?" she asked, ignoring the presence of her father and Lily.

"Me personally, no." Bryce looked down at her and everyone in the room could see what it cost him to add, "But as the sheriff, I've got a job to do."

"Fine, *Sheriff*," Mari said shortly. "I'll get my purse."

Bryce followed Mari out and down the hall, leaving Ron and Lily alone, standing in stunned silence.

She sucked in a gulp of air, then blew it out in a rush before saying, "This is ridiculous. Mari's no more guilty of selling drugs than I am."

Ron squeezed her hand again, then let her go, walking to stare out her window at the sun, slowly moving lower in the sky. Twilight wasn't far off. Soon the first stars would be winking into existence, even as the sun painted brilliant, vibrant streaks of color across the western sky.

Lily watched him, unsure of what to say, do. She'd never had children, so she couldn't imagine what must be going through Ron's mind. But she *did* love Mari like a daughter. The woman was everything Lily would have wanted a child of hers to be. Giving, loving, kind and generous to a fault. She was no criminal. But beneath the fury Mari must be feeling at the moment, there was undoubtedly fear.

"You should go be with her," Lily said softly.

He glanced at her and smiled wryly. "Oh, I want to," he admitted quietly. "That's always been my first instinct when someone attacks one of my children. Go in swinging and ask questions later."

"You're a good father, then."

"I'd like to think so."

Worry shadowed his eyes, and his features were grim. "But if I go in with Mari while she answers a few questions, then I'll be giving Bryce's suspicions more weight.''

She took a step toward him, then stopped. ''Oh, I don't know…''

Fury shot across his eyes like heat lightning, dissipating almost as quickly as it had come. ''Damn it, Bryce knows she's innocent. He's loved Mari for too long to believe otherwise.''

''Times change,'' Lily said, haunted by the fact that she'd said the same thing to him a little while ago—for a very different purpose.

''Times, yes,'' Ron said and walked back to her side. ''People, no. Whatever else Bryce is thinking, I know that deep down, that boy is convinced of Mari's innocence. If I didn't believe that, I'd go crazy.''

Amazed, Lily looked up at him. ''So you're not going to call your lawyers for her?''

''Oh, I'm calling the lawyers,'' he said, giving her a wicked smile. ''I trust Bryce…I just don't trust trumped-up evidence.'' The smile faded, and a look of pure determination etched itself onto his features. ''Somebody somewhere is going to a lot of trouble to make Mari look guilty.''

The simple clarity of that statement hit her like a load of bricks dropped on top of her head. ''Oh my God. I hadn't even considered that.''

''I've been thinking of nothing else lately.'' He gave her a sad smile. ''I hate to think that someone local is doing this to my girl. But it's the only thing that makes sense."

Strange, but now that he'd said it, little wheels in her head started clicking into place. Like pieces of a puzzle, shoved around on a tabletop until finally, with happenstance, the pieces fell into the right place. "In a twisted sort of way, you're right."

"Thank you."

"Hmm?" Her brain still reeling from the implications of Ron's theory, she hardly heard him. "For what?"

Ron lifted one hand and stroked the backs of his fingers down her cheek. "For once again stepping up to bat for my family. You seem to be doing that a lot lately."

She shrugged. "I was just—"

His thumb moved to rest atop her lips, cutting her off and silencing her completely. "Thank you."

She smiled against his touch. "You're welcome."

Nodding, he let his hand drop to his side again. Blowing out a breath, he said, "I'd better be going, I guess. See you in two hours."

She turned and watched him head for the door. "You still want to go to dinner?"

He stopped in the threshold and turned the power of his gaze on her. "I can't help Mari by sitting at home and stewing about this on my own. And if I am at home alone, I'll have more time to think, and that'll just worry me more."

"So I'm therapy, in a way?"

"You could say that." He grinned at her, but the smile didn't completely lift the shadows still lurking in his eyes. "After all, you did promise to de-sturdy me, remember, Ms. Cunningham?"

"I remember, Mr. Bingham."

"Then you can start on our date."

"On our date," she agreed.

Funny, but the word *date* had never sounded so...exciting before. Even as she thought it, Lily warned herself to dial it down a notch. She could enjoy the affair she planned to have with the handsome widower. But she wouldn't allow her heart to get all twisted up in something that wouldn't—couldn't—last.

A new trickle of excitement rolled through her body and smashed her defenses as his gaze dipped up and down, taking her in before finally lifting to look into her eyes again.

"Two hours."

Then he was gone.

And Lily's knees went so weak, she had to drop onto the edge of her desk to keep from falling.

Chapter Eight

The phone was ringing when Lily ran into her house with nothing more than a shower on her mind. She thought about ignoring the shrill ring. After all, wasn't that why God invented answering machines?

She toed off her tennis shoes and kicked them into the corner of the living room. There'd be time enough tomorrow to put them away. Right now she needed all the time she could get to turn herself from a substitute right fielder into a dinner date.

The phone rang again, taunting her.

What if it was Mari, she thought, imagining the younger woman might very well be sitting in Bryce's office, using up her one phone call.

"Oh, for heaven's sake, Lily," she said aloud, "you've been watching way too much TV." Why would Mari call Lily when she could call her father? Or her grandmother?

Yanking off her sweatshirt and already reaching behind her for the clasp of her bra, Lily counted the fourth ring and knew the machine would pick up on the fifth. She couldn't stand it. Never had been one of those people to screen calls. It seemed so...underhanded somehow. An if-you're-worthy-I'll-answer sort of thing. Besides, bottom line—she simply couldn't stand to leave a ringing phone unanswered.

Snatching it up, she said, "Hello?"

"Well, my goodness, you sound as though you've been running across the mountains."

Lily grabbed her sweatshirt and held it in front of her. Not that it mattered. Myrtle Bingham, the grand dame of Binghamton, founder of the Merlyn County Regional Hospital and the Janice Foster Memorial Midwifery Clinic, and Ron's mother, *couldn't* be appalled by Lily's outfit. But it was the principle of the thing. And Lily firmly hoped that video phones would *never* become popular.

"Hello, Myrtle." She smiled as she added, "I just walked in the door."

"Well then, good timing on my part. I wanted to speak to you about the fund-raiser you're planning for the research facility, Lily. If you don't mind, I'd like to know how the plans are coming along."

"Oh, I don't mind at all," she said, her brain instantly switching gears from date night back to business. Lily really liked Myrtle. A true lady in the best possible sense, Myrtle had spent her life as a philanthropist, devoting herself to both her family and to making life in Merlyn County, Kentucky, a little better.

At seventy-eight, Myrtle was a force of nature. Sweet, soft-spoken and invariably kind to everyone, the matriarch of the Bingham family had survived her share of tragedies over the years. But through it all, she'd maintained a quiet dignity and a loving nature that Lily admired and envied.

It had been Myrtle who'd begun the midwifery clinic, after one of her closest friends had died for want of good medical care. It had been Myrtle who'd cajoled and twisted the arms of old family friends into donating the money to keep the clinic well supplied. And it was Myrtle who kept on top of every little thing concerning *her* clinic.

"Would tomorrow suit you?" the older woman asked. "You could come to the house for tea."

Lily smiled to herself. Tea at Myrtle Bingham's house was only slightly less fabulous than tea at the Waldorf Astoria in New York. "That would be wonderful. I'd love to."

The Silhouette Reader Service™ — Here's how it works:

If offer card is missing write to: Silhouette Reader Service, 3010 Walden Ave., P.O. Box 1867, Buffalo NY 14240-1867

BUSINESS REPLY MAIL
FIRST-CLASS MAIL   PERMIT NO. 717-003   BUFFALO, NY

POSTAGE WILL BE PAID BY ADDRESSEE

SILHOUETTE READER SERVICE
3010 WALDEN AVE
PO BOX 1867
BUFFALO NY 14240-9952

NO POSTAGE
NECESSARY
IF MAILED
IN THE
UNITED STATES

"Excellent then. I'll see you at three. Goodbye, dear."

"Thank—" A dial tone burst into life in Lily's ear, and she grinned at the phone. Myrtle Bingham also didn't believe in wasting time.

Time.

Lily glanced at her watch and gulped. Five whole minutes gone. And with the shape she was in, she couldn't afford to waste five more. Peeling her clothes off as she went, she headed straight for the shower.

When she answered the door, Ron felt his breath leave him in a rush—as if he'd been sucker punched. His gaze locked on her and he gave her a quick up-and-down sweep. Her jaw-length blond hair curved under and she had one side tucked behind her left ear. Diamond earrings flashed at him in the glow of the porch light. She wore a dark red blouse with a wide, scooped neckline tucked into a short black skirt. The high-heeled black sandals on her feet only made her tanned and trim legs look even more amazing.

Her soft, floral scent floated on the night air, just before it reached his brain and fogged it entirely.

"Hello?" She smiled at him and finished him off.

"You look—" Ron shook his head and searched for an appropriate word. "—breathtaking."

Her smile brightened, though he wouldn't have thought that possible.

"That was worth waiting for," she said, and stepped onto her porch, pulling the front door closed behind her.

And with that one step, she was close. So close. He couldn't help himself. Before he could even think about it, Ron bent and claimed a brief kiss that sent jagged bits of flame tearing through him. The slightest touch of her mouth to his was enough to engulf him in a need he hadn't known in... Guilt pooled inside him in the space of a single heartbeat.

He'd *never* felt this hunger, this *pull*. Not even for Vi. And that admission cost him dearly. What he and Vi had shared had been...comfortable. Easy. The affection shared by people who had known each other most of their lives.

What he felt for Lily was quicksilver.

Lightning.

Heat.

And a hunger that threatened to consume him.

"Judging by your expression, I'm guessing that kiss didn't make you as happy as you thought it would," she said softly.

Ron sighed. "You have the annoying habit of being able to hit the nail squarely on the head every damn time."

"It's a gift."

Her eyes looked luminous in the glow of the overhead bulb. Deep, dark pools of temptation. Big and brown, her eyes haunted him, waking and sleeping, and it was only with effort these days that he remembered Violet's eyes had been blue. So dark a blue as to be almost purple. Hence, her name. He'd once thought he could live forever, just staring into Vi's eyes.

And now, he dreamed of dark-brown eyes…so different. So alluring.

What kind of man did that make him?

"Ron?"

Lily's voice crowded out his disturbing thoughts, and he told himself that self-examination was all well and good, but there was a time and place for it. Which this was *not*.

"Sorry," he said, and forced a smile until it felt almost natural. "Wool gathering."

"It's been a long time since I heard anyone use that phrase."

"I'm just an old-fashioned guy." Truer words were never spoken, he thought, taking her hand and leading her down the steps toward his car, which was waiting in the driveway. "Your flowers look nice."

She sighed and looked down at the cheerful pots of petunias. "They do, don't they?"

"And this depresses you?"

"Only momentarily," she said, resignation clear in her tone. "They'll be dead long before we've bonded."

"Well that's looking on the bright side."

"Oh," she said, smiling up at him, "what's the old saying…I've seen the enemy and he is me? Well, you're looking at the world's worst gardener."

"Me, too," he said on a laugh, pleased to be back on easy footing. "I was never allowed to mow a lawn. Vi used to say—" He caught himself and shut up fast. Nothing like talking about your late wife while you were out on a date with a woman you wanted to get in your bed.

Lily stopped dead and tugged at his hand to make him stop with her. Looking up at him, she met his gaze squarely before saying, "It's okay to talk about your wife, you know."

"I didn't mean to—"

"For heaven's sake, Ron," she said, "neither of us is a kid. We both have pasts. It would be foolish to pretend we didn't."

True. Every word was certainly true. But it didn't change the way he felt, talking about Vi with her. It was a weird sensation. One he hadn't had to deal with in ten years. The other women he'd seen had been— from the outset—temporary. But Lily wasn't like anyone else he'd ever known. She sure as hell wasn't a temporary kind of woman. Which was a damn shame, because that's the only kind he was interested in these days.

"How's Mari?" she asked as he opened the car door for her.

Ron stared at her. She sneaked up on a man, he thought. Never let him stay on his guard. And she *cared.* It had been too long since he'd been with someone who cared about what was happening in his life.

"She's okay," he said. "I talked to her just before I left my place. She's home from the station. Bryce isn't pressing charges."

"I should hope not."

He gave her a quick grin in appreciation of her hot defense. "Mari's furious but, I think, more hurt than angry. She's having a hard time coming to grips with the way Bryce is treating her."

"Not surprising. She loved him."

"Oh, she surely did." Ron smiled softly and shook his head. "The only thing that was able to pry Mari from Bryce's side was the thought of medical school."

"I take it our sheriff didn't approve."

"He wasn't the sheriff then," Ron said, remembering back to a time that was easier, quieter. "But no, he didn't approve. He wanted Mari to stay here and marry him."

"Uh-huh." Lily laid her hand on top of his. "So he felt threatened when she left—then forgotten when she came back."

Ron's gaze narrowed on her. He stared until she shifted uneasily from foot to foot. "Are you sure you're not psychic?"

She laughed and the sound was music. "I'm not psychic, trust me," she said, sliding onto the butter-soft, beige leather seat of his car. "Although," she added with a sigh as she looked around the interior of the elegant sedan, "I would have been willing to bet that your car interior would be beige."

"Another sign of sturdyism?"

"Oh, definitely."

"Looks like you've got your work cut out for you, then," he said, "doesn't it?"

Ron closed the car door and went around to the driver's side. He didn't even notice he was whistling.

Lily wasn't sure what she'd been expecting. But Big Jim's All You Can Eat Barbecue hadn't been on the top of her list. Or *anywhere* on her list, for that matter. Until tonight, she'd never heard of it. Of course, it was about an hour outside of Binghamton, and she hadn't exactly been doing a lot of exploring in the past few months.

"What do you think?" Ron parked the car, turned the engine off and stared through the windshield at the log building in front of them.

"It's very...*interesting*," Lily finally said, settling on an adjective that wasn't a compliment *or* an insult.

Big Jim's was constructed of rough-hewn logs, notched at the corners of the building. It could have passed as Daniel Boone's fort...but for the flash of brilliant-yellow neon over the double front door.

There was a wide porch, dotted with what looked like hand-carved rocking chairs, just in case a customer wanted to sit awhile. Lamplight and candlelight sparkled through the windows that spanned the length of the building, adding to the glow of neon proudly spelling out Big Jim's name.

"Interesting, huh?" Ron chuckled and got out of the car. Walking around to her side, he opened the door for her, then helped her out of the car. "So I'm guessing you didn't figure a sturdy man would come to a joint like this."

"Well, I did mention that I saw hope for you."

He grinned, and Lily's heart did a quick two step. "So you did," he said.

"Come here often?" Lily asked, enjoying the feel of her hand in his.

"More often than I used to."

Which meant what exactly, she wondered. Did he come here now because Vi had hated the place? Or was this a pilgrimage visit to a place his late wife had loved and shared with him?

What does it matter? Hadn't she been the one to say that they both had pasts? And in a county the size of Merlyn, they were bound to go places that he'd been with Vi. So why, she thought now with an inner groan, was she suddenly worried about competing with a dead woman?

"You like country music?" he asked, and closed the car door.

She plastered a smile on her face. "I've been in Kentucky for months. Country music won me over."

"You'll like the band here, then."

A band?

This evening wasn't turning out as she'd thought it would. When Ron invited her to dinner, Lily had assumed they'd drive into Lexington and have drinks and a civilized meal at a four-star restaurant. Instead, they were...here.

Ron Bingham was becoming more and more of a surprise. Apparently there were far more layers to him than she ever would have guessed.

Lily ran her palms down the front of her full, black skirt, then fiddled with the collar of her dark red blouse and clutched her red leather bag. Tipping her head back, she smiled up at him. "I can't wait."

He studied her for a long minute, then smiled to himself. "Uh-huh." He took her arm, threading it through the crook of his as he led the way across the gravel lot. His hand was firm on hers, keeping her steady as her fashionable, but completely useless, sandals slipped and slid on the loose gravel.

Their footsteps crunched companionably and they

almost seemed to move in time to the rhythm of the music drifting from inside the restaurant.

Glancing to one side, Lily covertly took another look at the man beside her. Ron wore faded jeans and a dark-green, collared pullover shirt. His dusty brown boots looked worn and comfortable. Obviously, away from his office and his workday world he was more relaxed than she'd ever given him credit for.

He didn't look the least bit stodgy tonight. He looked…like a cowboy.

And she felt completely overdressed. For just a second or two, she flashed back to her past and felt the old, soul-shaking sensation of not fitting in. Her scoop-necked blouse and billowing skirt were as out of place at Big Jim's Barbecue as her too-loud charm bracelet would be in church. And yet, hadn't she convinced herself years ago not to worry about fitting in? To be herself and let the rest of the world take care of itself?

Ignoring the noisy little voice in the back of her mind, Lily said, "It looks crowded."

"Popular spot." He cast her a quick, sideways look. "Not your kind of place?"

"Hard to tell without having seen it."

"It only gets better on the inside."

"Good." She could tell he didn't believe her. He was no doubt waiting for her to turn her nose up and ask him to take her to the closest French restaurant.

Just as she'd expected him to take her somewhere quiet and elegant. So. Even though they'd shared a couple of amazing kisses and were contemplating a whole lot more, he didn't know her at all. Apparently, any more than she knew him.

He was still watching her and waiting for her to turn into the society matron he assumed she was.

But she'd been surprising people her whole life. She could handle one crabby, deadly attractive man.

His eyebrows lifted slightly, as they climbed the steps to the porch. His boot heels clacked on the scarred wooden planks. He stopped short, yanked one of the doors open and held it for her.

A wall of sound poured out and flew past them into the night. Guitars wept, a fiddle sighed and a singer poured his soul into a ballad that soared through the rafters of the log building. When the music abruptly ended a moment later, applause roared through the place, sounding like a freight train speeding down the tracks.

Sawdust littered the wood floor, and a few dozen round tables were scattered around the huge room. Candlelight flickered from the center of every table and sparkled from the wagon-wheel chandeliers hanging from the overhead beams. The crowd was loud but friendly. Waitresses in blue jeans and blue-and-white-checked shirts carried huge trays filled with mountains of food. A gleaming, mahogany bar took up the whole far wall, and several customers sat on high stools in front of it. At the back of the room was a stage, and in front of it, a wide but crowded dance floor. On the stage the band was tuning up for their next number.

"Hi, I'm Sandy," a perky blond with a wildly swinging ponytail announced as she walked up to them and grinned. "Two of you for dinner tonight?"

She showed them to a table, left them menus, then bounced off to greet the next customers.

Lily simply stared at the laminated menu. She hadn't thought it possible that so many different items could be barbecued.

"Lost?"

"Just a little," she admitted, looking at him over the top of her menu.

"Trust me?"

She studied him. "Should I?"

"When it comes to barbecue? Absolutely."

"All right." She handed him the menu and said, "It's up to you."

When their waitress, a woman slightly less perky than Sandy, stopped by, Ron ordered two plates of ribs and a pitcher of beer.

"This is a whole new side of you," Lily said thoughtfully after the waitress was gone again.

"Think I was born in a three-piece suit?"

"I guess I did."

"So, the great Lily can be wrong at times, eh?"

"It's been known to happen," she said, her mouth twitching slightly. "Rarely, but yes."

"It's good to know you can be surprised."

"Oh, you surprise me all the time," she admitted, speaking just loud enough to be heard over the singer's beautiful voice.

"Really? How?"

What could she say? That she was surprised that a bearded, usually crabby man had the power to shadow her dreams and make sleep nearly impossible? Oh, no. A woman just did not give a man that kind of ammunition.

So she ignored his question entirely. "I wouldn't have thought you were the kind of man to own a pair of cowboy boots."

"There's a lot you don't know about me, Lily."

"I'm beginning to see that."

"Care to learn?"

"That's why I'm here."

"Is *that* the reason?"

"Why else?"

He smiled. "The de-sturdying process?"

She laughed. "That might not take as long as originally thought."

"Happy to hear it," he said, and pushed up from the chair. "While we wait for our beer, how about a dance, Ms. Lily?"

One blond eyebrow lifted. "You like the saloon hall sound of that, don't you?"

"I'll be your cowboy and you can be my Ms. Lily," he offered, still holding his hand out, waiting for her to take it.

"Role playing?" she asked, slipping her hand into his as she stood up. "Why Ron Bingham, I think there's hope for you yet."

He only smiled again. "Dance with me."

She stared up at him. Candlelight flickered in his dark hair and shone in his eyes. All around them, people laughed and talked and drank and conversations rose and fell like the tides. But it was as if they were alone, just the two of them. His gaze slammed hard into her and left her nearly breathless.

Lily looked from his eyes to his hand and back again. His smile warmed her while his eyes sent heat spiraling through her body to finally pool in the pit of her stomach. This man was so much more than she'd thought. And she was in much deeper trouble than she'd ever expected.

Chapter Nine

As a dancer, Lily didn't know her right foot from her left. But she had so much fun in the attempt, Ron got a kick out of watching her laugh. Her eyes shone and her laughter rang out over the music, adding a layer to the entertainment he'd never experienced before.

As a two-step flowed into a ten-step, she valiantly tried to keep up, but mostly succeeded in sliding her feet across the floor, just to keep pace with him. And finally, when the band played another ballad, Ron pulled her into his arms and led her in a soft sway that filled him with a longing that was as new and exciting as it was dangerous.

"Having fun?" he asked, staring down into her eyes.

She shook her hair back from her face, and the diamonds at her ears winked at him. "It's terrific," she said, then glanced over her shoulder and excused herself to the guy she bumped into while making a turn. "This place is great."

She meant it. He could see the truth in her eyes, and a part of him was surprised…again. Why that was so, he didn't know. Nothing about her should still be surprising him. He'd brought her to Big Jim's, expecting that her Bar Harbor upbringing would kick in and her small straight nose would go up in the air with a haughty sniff.

Didn't make any sense to feel that way and he knew it. In the time Lily'd been in Binghamton, she hadn't once displayed the "society girl" attitude he kept expecting. Instead, she'd made herself a part of Merlyn County. She'd made a home and friends and slipped into the slower way of life as if she'd been born to it.

But she hadn't been born to it.

A big part of Ron was simply waiting for her to tire of her country experiment and head back to the big city. And if she did, he realized with a start, he'd miss her. A lot.

She tipped her head to one side, and her hair swung

in a golden arc. "You didn't expect me to like it, did you?"

Guilt slapped at him. "Guess not."

Her eyes narrowed thoughtfully, but she didn't stop dancing, didn't try to inch out of the tight hold he had on her. "Was this a test of some kind?"

Ron winced and let his gaze slide briefly past her to the band, as if looking for help, before shifting it back to her. "*Test* is a strong word."

"But accurate?"

He tightened the arm he had wrapped around her waist, just in case she suddenly took it into her head to bolt. The music played and the other couples kept time, moving around the dance floor in an unrehearsed, clockwise pattern.

Lying to her was unacceptable. Not only did it go against his personal grain, but Lily was no fool. She'd spot it in a second and then the hole he'd found himself in would only get deeper.

"Let's say I was wondering how you'd react."

Her mouth tightened slightly. "Let's say you stop doing that."

He lifted one shoulder in a helpless shrug. "Can't. You're a mystery, Lily."

She laughed at that and Ron relaxed his grip on her, no longer worried that she would take off. He'd figured she'd be furious. Just another little piece of the mystery.

"There's not a thing mysterious about me."

"Depends on your point of view," he said, and led her in a spin designed to keep her off balance.

"Maybe you're just looking for a mystery."

"Meaning?"

"Meaning, if I'm a mystery, I become safer."

A boom of laughter shot from him before he could stop it. Several of the dancers stared at him, but he ignored them. "Hell, Lily. There's *nothing* safe about you."

She sniffed, but he could tell she was almost pleased by his statement. One corner of her mouth lifted slightly before she could tame it into submission.

"Some women might take that as a compliment," she said after a long second or two.

"They'd be right."

Now she *did* smile, and as she did, she moved in closer to him, until he felt the hard tips of her nipples pressing hotly into his chest like tiny brands. It had been years since his body had embarrassed him in public...but damned if he didn't feel like a randy teenager.

"Well then, thank you," she said.

"Oh, you're welcome."

She moved into him until he thought his breath might stop. His body reacted, and he knew she was well aware of the fact by the way her eyes darkened and her breathing quickened. One blond eyebrow lifted as she leaned into him more fully, pressing her body along his until every inch of him ached.

She moved her hand from his shoulder to the back of his head, and he felt the soft slide of her fingers through his hair. An intimate gesture that touched him even as it fired his soul.

Under cover of the music, she whispered, ''Do we really have to stay for dinner?''

Ron's heart jumped. He moved his right hand down her spine to her bottom and then he simply held her, pressed tightly to the erection hardened between them. Her eyes flashed, and she surreptitiously rocked her hips against him in sensual promise, making him even crazier than he already was.

She felt so good. So warm and willing, and she looked so beautiful, she was enough to tempt a saint out of Heaven. And God knew he was no saint.

When he could speak past the tight knot of desire lodged in his throat, he gruffly answered, ''We'll need dinner.''

Disappointment shimmered in her eyes and made him feel like a damn king.

''Why?''

He smiled. ''You'll need your strength.''

''We'll go to my place.'' Ron's words were sharp, clipped, as if simply speaking had required all of his self-control.

Lily knew just how he felt.

Staying at the restaurant, eating a dinner she didn't even taste, waiting for the check to be picked up, walking out to the parking lot…it was all a waste. A waste of precious time. A delay that had her body burning and her mind swimming with images of hot, naked bodies twisting together on crisp, clean sheets.

"Your place," she echoed, gaze glued to the dark road ahead, as if she could hurry them along just by concentrating.

"Closer," he murmured, and steered the car around a mountainous curve. "And—"

"And?" She turned her head to look at him. Even his silhouette ratcheted up the need clawing at her. She wanted to reach for him. Stroke his hair, trace her fingers along his jaw, then slide down his body, learning every hard plane and sculpted muscle.

She curled her fingers into a fist.

He glanced at her before turning his gaze back to the two-lane road. "I don't have any condoms with me."

"Oh." She laughed shortly, then simply smiled. "No worry about pregnancy, you know."

He smiled, too, she saw it, in the reflected light of the dashboard. "Thank God," he muttered. "But there are other—"

"Oh." Stupid. She was a woman of the world. She

knew darn well that there were far scarier things out there than a simple unplanned pregnancy. And a curl of warmth threaded its way through her at the realization that he was still thinking clearly enough to want to protect her.

She had it bad.

Lily closed her eyes briefly, then opened them to stare blindly at the twin slashes of brightness thrown from the headlights. She'd known for weeks that she *wanted* Ron, from a purely sexual point of view. What she hadn't counted on was feeling anything else.

And if she wasn't completely off base here—and she knew she wasn't—she was already halfway in love with the man. Which probably wasn't a good thing.

She'd never succeeded at love before.

Every single attempt at anything more than passion had only resulted in a painful lesson in disappointment. And there was no reason to suspect that this situation with Ron would be any different. Even while her blood boiled and her body hummed in anticipation, her heart realized the danger and braced itself.

He didn't want love.

He'd already had love.

With his late wife.

So where did that leave her? Lily thought.

"Don't think," he blurted out suddenly in the strained silence.

"What?" She turned her head to look at him.

He spared her a glance, then was forced to concentrate on not wrapping them around a tree. "I said, don't think."

"About what?"

"About anything."

"Tall order."

"Not really," he said, and took his right hand from the steering wheel to reach across the space separating them.

"Ron…"

"Don't think, Lily," he said again, softer this time as his hand rested on her thigh.

She felt the heat of his touch drift down deep inside her, warming, then scalding her as his hand moved on her leg, inching the hem of her skirt up higher, higher.

She inhaled sharply and looked down at her lap, watching him touch her. Shadowy light illuminated them both and when his hand slipped beneath the hem of her skirt and touched her bare thigh, she hissed in a breath through clenched teeth.

"Still thinking?" he murmured.

"Uh-huh." Thinking that if he touched her a little higher, she just might implode.

"Can't have that." His voice was a low rush of

sound, just barely decipherable above the hum of the tires on the asphalt.

A cool stream of air-conditioned air blew at them from the vents, but it couldn't help with the fires consuming Lily. Nothing could.

She twisted in her seat, but the belt across her chest and lap held her firmly in place while Ron ran his hand up the inside of her thigh. His fingers dusted lightly across her skin, and she opened her legs wider to invite him in.

Her brain took a vacation.

But her body beat her to it.

"No thinking allowed tonight, Lily," he said, his voice tight now, with a hunger she recognized as a reflection of her own. "Just feeling."

"Ron..."

"I can't wait," he said, moving his hand higher on her leg until he was just a touch away from her aching center.

She choked out a laugh. "We're gonna crash and die if you keep this up."

His own laugh sounded strained, almost painful. "No dying allowed until I've touched you."

Then he did.

"Oh..." Lily couldn't contain the gasp, couldn't pretend control. His fingers smoothed over the heart of her and she wanted to weep with the joy of it.

Even through the fragile silk of her panties, she felt

his heat swamping her and she ached to lift her hips into his touch. But she was caught. Trapped. Nowhere to move. Nothing to do but sit there and let him explore her body.

Her hands curled over the edge of the seat even as her legs opened wider, offering him access. Offering herself to the man whose hands contained such incredible heat.

"Ron…" She was so close to a climax. Her breath caught in her chest. She willed herself to take the climb toward release. It had been so long since she'd felt this magic. And even then, it had been nothing like this.

Scandalous, a niggling voice in the back of her mind whispered.

Good, she wanted to shout back.

A little scandal was a good thing.

And what Ron was doing to her went *way* beyond good.

With one hand on the wheel, he maneuvered the steep mountain road and the danger implicit in what he—*they*—were doing only made it that much more exciting. She felt young and reckless. Wild and unstoppable.

His clever fingers pulled at the edge of her panties, trying to get beneath the scrap of silk to touch flesh. Lily heard herself say thickly, "Tear them."

He groaned and did it.

She heard the fabric rip.

Felt it give.

Then felt the cool, air-conditioned air blowing on her hot flesh like a salve. But an instant later his hand was on her again, and heat welled up fresh and blistering.

He touched her, fingers dipping into her warmth, claiming her, taking her higher and faster than she'd ever been before. She squirmed, trying to move into him, and was held prisoner by the seat belt pinning her in place. Frustration pooled inside her, then bubbled over as she tried again and again to lift her hips into his hand. All she could do was keep herself open to him. To the strokes and caresses designed to drive her insane.

"Ron. Ron…"

"Come, Lily," he urged quietly, his voice a tight thread that snaked across the car for her. "Let go and come."

"I want to," she said, letting her head fall back on the seat as sensation after sensation coursed inside her, pushing her farther along on the road to perfection. "Oh, I want it. I need it."

Outside the car, summer lightning flashed in the clouds overhead, and the distant roar of thunder sounded like a caged beast demanding release.

Just how Lily felt.

His thumb brushed her most sensitive spot and she

nearly shrieked. She slapped her hands tighter on the edge of the leather seats and squeezed until she was half afraid her long nails would puncture the soft material and dig right into the padding.

Then he touched her deeply, thrusting two fingers inside her damp heat and Lily felt the top of her head blow off. The first contraction rippled deep within her and she rode it fiercely, giving herself up to the ride and the well of spiraling amazement that shot through her like one of the skyward blasts of lightning.

She closed her eyes, called his name breathlessly and lost herself in the tumult crashing inside her. And as she slowly sank back to earth, his touch was still there, still on her, still within her, cradling her, easing her back to where breathing was possible.

"Oh, my…" It was the best she could manage. And even at that, the two little words were a triumph. Her body still rippled and shuddered, and his hand, warm at her center, kept her grounded yet ready for the next trip into wonder.

"Damn," Ron muttered thickly, steering the car adroitly through another sharp curve, "tell me why I brought you to a restaurant so far from my place."

Lily laughed and felt it bubble from her throat like fine champagne. Turning her head on the seat back to watch him, she said, "Because it gives us so much more time to practice?"

He shot her a quick look, and the raw hunger in

his gaze reached out and caught her in a trap more binding than the seat belt still notched tightly across her body. Breath labored, he nodded sharply and said, "A lot to be said for a good practice session."

"My thoughts exactly," she said on a sigh of completion.

"Glad you feel that way."

"What's not to like?" She hadn't been this relaxed, this...unwound in months.

"You know what they say, though," he said, his voice still rough with desire.

"What?"

"Practice makes perfect."

"Sure, but—" She broke off as his thumb stroked her again. "Ron..."

"Lily," he said, scraping the pad of his thumb across a single sensitive spot, "shut up."

She hissed in a short breath and held it. "Right."

It was a long ride back to Ron's house.

Three and a half climaxes to be exact.

By the time he pulled the car into the driveway at his condo, Ron's body was on full alert, and he could hardly draw breath. It was a miracle they hadn't been killed on the highway.

But once he'd started touching her, he couldn't have stopped if his life had depended on it. Her responses, her sighs, the way her body contracted around his fingers when she climaxed only made him want more. Stolen glances in the soft light of the dashboard had only fed the fires consuming him. He watched his hand on her. Saw her body open for him and wanted more than anything else in his life to push his body into hers. To claim what he'd been dreaming about, thinking about, for months.

He had to have her.

Naked and under him.

Over him.

Surrounding him.

And he had to have her *now*.

He hit the garage button, pulled the car inside, threw it into gear and shut the engine off. As the automatic garage door hummed into life, shutting them in, she was already undoing her seat belt. He dealt with his quickly, then half turned in the seat, reached for her and pulled her onto his lap.

He couldn't wait. Not another minute. Not another second. He had to taste her.

His mouth came down on hers and she parted her lips for him in a sweet rush of hunger that clawed at him. Their tongues twisted, mated, plunging in and out of each other's mouths, tasting, exploring, driving the need between them to even higher peaks.

He tugged at her blouse, pulling it free of the waistband of her skirt, and in seconds his right hand swept beneath the hem of the silky material. He cupped her breast and even through the lacy fabric of her bra, he fingered her nipple and relished her soft groan.

More.

He tore his mouth from hers and stared down at her through half-crazed eyes. "Lily, I need you, *bad.*"

Breathing hard, the pulse at the base of her throat pounding, she reached up, caught his face between her palms and pulled his head down for another long, hard kiss. When she released him again, she only said, *"Now."*

Nodding, he muttered, "Come on, then."

He pushed the car door open, then climbed out, still holding on to her. When he set her on her feet, she wobbled unsteadily, then grabbed him to maintain her balance. "Legs are a little rubbery." She threw her hair out of her eyes and gave him a wicked grin. "Your fault."

He grinned back. "My fault, so I'll fix it."

Bending down, he swept her up into his arms and headed for the connecting door to the kitchen.

"Wow." She laughed aloud and kicked her legs like an old movie star. "No one's ever carried me before."

"Good to know I'm the first," he said, opening the door and stalking through. A man on a mission, he never slowed down. He went through the kitchen, down the hallway and then up the stairs to the bedroom. Need tore at him. Hunger reared up and chewed on him. Every cell in his body was screaming for the release he could only find in her arms.

In her body.

Lily opened the buttons on his shirt and skimmed one hand across his chest.

Ron sucked in a gulp of air and swallowed it, half afraid it might be the last easy one he'd be able to take.

He kicked the partially opened bedroom door and sent it crashing into the wall. He didn't care. Hell, he didn't care if a tornado touched down—as long as he first had the chance to bury himself in Lily's warmth.

Striding to the bed, he kept a tight grip on her and bent down to grab the comforter. Tossing it to the foot of the bed, he then dropped Lily onto the mattress and smiled tightly when she laughed and bounced.

"Practice is over," he said, reaching for the top drawer on the bedside table.

"Then let's get going," she answered. Sitting up, she pulled her blouse up and over her head, then fingered the front clasp of her bra. Her breasts spilled free, and Ron's mouth watered at the sight of her.

She sat caught in the silvery moonlight and looked like some wild nature nymph. Her black skirt pooled around her, and as she shimmied out of it, he lost what was left of that breath he'd been saving.

His heart jumped as she toed off her sandals, then leaned back on her hands, watching him. Not a shred of modesty about her, thank heaven. And she didn't have a thing to be modest about. Her body was just as a woman's should be. Full and lush and curvy. The kind of body most men dreamed about touching.

And for tonight she was all his.

With that thought in mind, he tore off his own clothes, grabbed a handful of foil packets and tossed them onto the bed.

Lily glanced at them, then turned that wicked smile of hers back on him. "I *love* a confident man."

Chapter Ten

The word *love* seemed to hover in the air like an unwanted bee at a picnic.

Ron's chest constricted and he fought for breath. No one had said anything about *love*. And he didn't want this to be about love. This was raw, pulsating hunger. Need driving two consenting adults into an affair that would be mutually satisfying.

This wasn't about *love*.

Seconds ticked past, and he simply stood there, staring down at the woman who had been driving him insane for months. She waited, warm, lush, naked, and as he looked at her, he saw anxiety and hesitation blossom in her eyes. The one thing he didn't want.

"You all right?" she asked.

"Why don't I show you?" he answered, and joined her on the bed.

Shadows still clouded her dark-brown eyes as she hitched a breath and met his gaze. "Ron—"

"No." He cupped her face with his palm and shook his head. "No worrying tonight. No *thinking* tonight."

She laughed a little. "It's not an easy thing to shut my brain down."

Ron smiled and leaned into her. *"Watch me."*

He kissed her. Long and deep and warm, he took her mouth and gave her everything inside him that had been waiting for just this opportunity. His mouth claimed hers, his tongue demanded entry, and when she surrendered, he stroked her heat with hungry caresses that had her sighing into him.

He slid his hand from her face, down her throat and across her chest to touch first one breast, then the other. She moaned from the back of her throat and arched into him, half lifting from the mattress to press herself against him. His thumb and forefinger tweaked her nipples, inflaming them both with the teasing touch.

Breaking the kiss, Ron lifted his head and looked at her through eyes glazed with a passion that was singeing him. "Gorgeous," he muttered thickly, pleased that he'd been able to get that one word past the knot of need pulsing in his throat.

She laughed, a soft, low chuckle that rippled through the air and settled over him like a gift. "Gorgeous? Now there speaks an eager man."

He smiled and let his hand sweep along her body. "Trust me on this. I said gorgeous. I mean gorgeous."

Something in her eyes flickered, and she reached up for him, scraping her palms across his chest. He sucked in air through clenched teeth.

"You know something?" she said, lifting her gaze to meet his. "You're not so bad yourself."

He grinned at her, feeling everything inside him spark to life. Then he lowered his head to kiss her once more, briefly, passionately, before shifting, letting his lips trail along her jaw, down her throat. He wanted to taste all of her, to mark her body with his mouth as if branding her.

Tonight she was *all*.

Tonight the world existed in a pair of warm brown eyes and welcoming arms.

Tonight he finally had Lily exactly where he'd wanted her for so long.

"Ron..." His name drifted from her lips as she writhed beneath him, caught, trapped by his ministrations.

"Let me have you, Lily," he said, his breath dusting across her flesh just before his lips and tongue found first one nipple, then the other.

"You *had* me," she whispered brokenly. "On the ride over here, remember?"

"More," he murmured, drawing her nipple into his mouth and suckling her with exquisitely torturous moves.

"Yes," she answered. *"More."*

He smiled against her breast and took her higher, sucking, drawing, pulling at her flesh until she twisted against him, moaning. He ran the edges of his teeth across the tip of her rigid nipple and drew a hiss of appreciation from her.

While he tasted her, indulging his need, his hand swept along her body, caressing her rib cage, her abdomen and then lower. Once more he touched her heat, the center of her need and the answer to his.

She opened for him, her legs falling wide, inviting a deeper caress, and he smiled again, despite the hunger now clawing at the base of his throat and echoing throughout his soul.

He dipped one finger into her depths, and she lifted her hips, rocking against his hand. His body tightened until he could hardly breathe. She ran one hand down his back, and he felt every one of her fingertips like a tiny match, skimming fire along his skin.

He cupped her, his hand covering her heat, his thumb stroking the sensitive bud that held the secrets to her climax. She practically jumped straight up at that small contact, and Ron lifted his head to look down at her.

"Not again," she whispered, licking her lips and shaking her head against the mattress.

"No?"

"No." She looked up at him and her eyes looked hazy, soft and unfocused. "You already gave me three with nothing for you."

One eyebrow lifted as he grinned at her. "Three and a half."

"But who's counting?"

"Me." Just remembering her passionate cries as he touched her on the ride here fueled the fires inside him until he could hardly breathe. "We didn't finish that last one—"

"Ron—"

"So I owe you the other half at least," he said, continuing his gentle assault with his fingertips.

"But…I…want…*you*…inside…me." Every word stood alone. Every word she managed to speak was a triumph of will.

"Soon," he promised, hoping he could hold out against his own need long enough to drive her over the edge again. Selfishly, he wanted to watch her eyes as she went over. He wanted to feel her body tremble. He wanted to be the man who could make her shatter.

He shifted, moving along her body, trailing lips and

hands, feeling her move and twist beneath him. He kissed every inch of her, luxuriating in the smooth, warm feel of her flesh beneath his lips. So lush, so full, not a sharp angle on her, he thought wildly, fiercely. She was a woman built for loving. Built for joining with a man and making him insane with hunger for her.

He kissed her belly, swirling his tongue into and out of her navel, just to hear her gasp. He smiled against her flesh, then kept going, lower, lower, until he knelt between her legs. Scooping his hands under her bottom, he lifted her from the mattress and held her, pinned like a butterfly to a board.

Meeting her gaze, he watched her eyes widen, then darken in anticipation.

"Ron, you don't—"

"Lily," he said, already bending his head toward her center, "you're talking again."

"Right."

She shut up fast and bit down hard on her bottom lip as his mouth claimed her. Lily tried to close her eyes and concentrate on the sensations pouring through her. But she couldn't help herself. She had to watch. Had to watch him take her in the most intimate fashion imaginable.

His tongue caressed her. He licked and stroked with exquisite care, pushing her higher and higher toward the peak she'd already reached so many times tonight. Lily's mind raced, her heart stuttered, her pulse pounded. She grabbed fistfuls of the sheet beneath her and held on as if afraid she might slide off the edge of the earth. But she was safe in Ron's strong hands. And tortured by his mouth.

She rode the wave cresting inside her and forgot about everything else except what was happening to her. Concentrating, focusing on the feelings mounting within, she kept her eyes open and watched him take her to the edge of the moon and then over. Lily screamed his name as she took the plunge and lay quivering in his grasp.

Before the last of her inner contractions were over, Ron eased her down onto the mattress, then grabbed up a condom and sheathed himself. Desire was a living, breathing thing inside him now. He needed Lily more than his next breath. Needed to be a part of her. To be buried so deeply inside her that he couldn't find his way out again. Needed to feel her close around him and hold him to her.

"Now," she whispered, reaching for him.

"Oh, yeah. Now."

In the moonlight spearing across the wide bed, she looked impossibly beautiful and completely irresistible. Her scent, a faint blend of flowers, reached for him, invading his senses, capturing him—mind, soul, heart.

He moved into her embrace and felt her hold him,

her arms wrapping around him tightly, pressing him to her as he pushed his body into hers. She lifted her legs, winding them around his hips and then moved with him, sliding instinctively into the ancient rhythm that bound all lovers into the same dance.

Together, they fed the flames consuming them. Lips met, tongues caressed, breath mingled and heartbeats raced in tandem. The healthy, wonderful sound of bodies meeting in the otherwise still room pushed them faster, harder toward completion.

Ron moved within her and felt a connection he hadn't known in far too long. Her body cradled his. Her soul met his. This felt...so right. So...good. Lily had somehow become more than need. She was now...*necessary*. And even as that thought darted quickly through his mind, he pushed it aside, forcing himself to concentrate only on the rocketing pleasure climbing within.

She reached around and cupped his cheek with her hand. He pulled her hand free, linked his fingers with hers. Joined together they found that peak and, together, fell over the edge.

Hours later Lily felt as though she'd been wrung dry of every emotion and sensation her body was capable of feeling.

She turned her head on the pillow and looked down toward the foot of the bed, where Ron lay sprawled, breath huffing from his chest. They'd worked their way around the king-size mattress as if it was a race-track. Once, she'd even fallen off the end of the bed to land on the thick, plush, beige carpet. But that hadn't slowed either of them down for long. Ron had simply joined her on the floor and hadn't missed a step in taking her to staggering new heights.

"Wow," she whispered and winced slightly. Her throat was dry, her mouth felt like cotton. If she thought she could stand up, she'd wander downstairs, find the kitchen and get something to drink.

But that wasn't going to happen.

She could hardly lift her eyelids.

"I was thinking the same thing," he muttered from the foot of the bed.

Lily smiled and felt as though it had cost her a great effort. "Your self-confidence was well placed." She swept one hand out lazily and encountered a pile of torn condom wrappers.

"I aim to please."

"Oh, I think it's safe to say you pulled that off."

"Same goes," he said, lifting one hand in salute before letting it drop to the mattress again.

Laughing to herself, Lily gathered her pitiful reserves of energy and pushed herself into a sitting position. Every muscle ached. Every cell in her body felt charged up and electrified. Her blood rushed expectantly through her veins, and deep in the core of her, sensitive skin awaited the next bout of delight.

Apparently, she was just as indefatigable as Ron. Which surprised the hell out of her. She'd never been that big a fan of sex. She'd always assumed she just didn't have much of a sex drive. After all, she'd managed to go very long stretches without being the least bit tempted.

But Ron was different.

He touched her, and she went up in flames.

He looked at her, and her body went liquid and welcoming.

He *stopped* touching her, and she wanted to scream in frustration.

Lily pushed one hand through her hair and wasn't surprised to find her fingers trembling. Heaven help her, she wanted him again.

"You'll have to give me a few minutes," he muttered.

"What?"

He sat up, too, and they were facing each other on the rumpled sheets. Reaching out one hand to her, he trailed his fingertips along her arm, then let them drift across her body to caress the tops of her breasts.

Lily sucked in a breath and shivered.

He smiled. "I said, if you keep looking at me like that, I'm gonna need a few minutes. Not as young as I used to be."

"You could have fooled me."

One corner of his mouth lifted higher. "To quote you…'You're not so bad yourself.'"

Lily laughed and slapped one hand across her mouth to muffle the sound.

"What's so funny?"

"It's so clichéd," she said when she finally got her laughter under control. "We're actually having the 'Was it good for you?' talk."

He laughed, too, and shook his head. "Well, someone has to have that talk, or it's not officially a cliché, is it?"

"I guess not."

Lily watched him and though she knew it was silly, since he was sitting right beside her, she felt him distance himself. There was nothing overt about it, and she was almost sure that he wasn't even aware of it. But still, it was there.

In the last few hours they'd been as close as too people could ever be. They'd explored every inch of each other's bodies and discovered what delights they held. Yet now that there was a pause in the festivities, there was a sense of discomfort quickly rising up between them like an invisible wall Lily had no idea how to scale.

Seconds of silence ticked past and Lily almost *felt* that wall grow another couple of inches. Funny, but she was sitting naked beside this man and felt as though she couldn't touch him.

"Lily—"

"Look—"

They both stopped, and that sense of uneasiness settled down between them.

"You first," he said, waving one hand in a half-hearted bow.

She inhaled sharply, then let the air rush from her lungs. "This was...*amazing*," she said, stepping carefully now as she hadn't all night. They'd moved together in a smooth rhythm, as if they'd done this dance many times before. Why now, when it was all over, did it feel awkward between them?

"Yeah, it was."

"Me first, remember?"

"You're right. Go ahead."

Great. She had the go-ahead. Now, if she only had the words.

"I might be wrong, but I'm picking up on a little...regret, coming from you."

One black eyebrow lifted, but he didn't deny it. Small consolation to be right in this instance.

"Not regret exactly," he said, and took her hand in his. Rubbing his thumb over her fingers, he looked down at their joined hands for a long moment before looking up at her again. "It's just that you surprised me again, Lily."

She took comfort from the feel of his hand on hers. "Yeah? How?"

He swallowed hard. "I didn't expect to *feel* so much," he admitted. "And I don't know what to do with it all."

"Why do you have to *do* anything with it?" she asked, watching his eyes, seeing the shadows play in the blue-green depths. She wished they weren't there, but since they were, better to deal with them outright. "Ron, we're two adults who wanted to spend the night together. It would have been pointless if we hadn't enjoyed it, wouldn't it?"

He smiled and squeezed her hand. "Yeah."

"This," she said, waving her free hand to indicate the wide bed and the two of them, naked in the center of it, "doesn't mean forever. It doesn't mean that you have to *do* anything beyond telling me how wonderful I am."

She said the last with a soft smile on her face and hoped he wouldn't notice just how much those casual words had cost her.

"That's easy enough," he said, and leaned in to dust a kiss at the corner of her mouth. Pulling back, just a breath, he whispered, "Lily, you're wonderful."

She shivered again.

Foolish heart, she thought as that organ jumped

into life. Hadn't her heart been broken enough in her lifetime? Hadn't it learned anything?

He stared deeply into her eyes and she knew the truth. Her heart would *never* learn to stop loving. To stop reaching for what she'd longed for most of her life.

It would be up to her to protect both her heart and the new life she'd built in Kentucky.

"Back atcha," she said, forcing a teasing note into her voice as she reached up and stroked his cheek with her fingertips. "I didn't even mind the beard— too much."

"Good to know." He pulled her into his arms, swinging her around to lie across his lap.

Cradled in his muscular arms, Lily stared up at him and tried to keep her heart from taking that one wild, last leap. She felt his heartbeat beneath her cheek and felt the strong grip of his hands on her body and knew she was fighting a losing battle. Still, she tried to warn herself to keep her emotions in check. To stick to the rules she'd set down for this affair.

But as his eyes met hers and his hands caressed her with long, tender strokes, Lily knew this was a war she would never win.

Her heart had taken the plunge already.

She was in love—*real* love—for the first time in her life.

With a man who still loved a ghost.

Sudden tears burned, and blurred her vision.

Then he dipped his head for another kiss, and Lily clung to him, pouring her heart and her newly discovered emotions into the meeting of their mouths. She gave him all she had, even knowing that he would never have taken it if he'd guessed the truth.

Their simple little affair was going to end up breaking Lily's heart.

Again.

Chapter Eleven

While sitting at her desk the next morning, the previous night's "activities" seemed almost like a dream. Like something that had happened to someone else. Until, of course, Lily tried to do something foolish like walk down the hall to fetch herself a cup of coffee. Then, as every muscle in her body ached and screamed with fatigue, she was forced to realize that yes, the night *had* happened.

Not that she didn't want to remember it all. Actually, she was fairly certain that every moment of the glorious night had been permanently etched into her brain. She just knew that when she was eighty she'd be able to close her eyes and remember the feel of Ron's lips on her body.

She only hoped the pain in her heart would have lessened by then.

Shaking her head, she grumbled, "For heaven's sake, Lily, stop being so melodramatic. It isn't the end of the world, you know."

"Who're you trying to convince?"

Lily gasped, slapped one hand to the bottom of her throat and forcibly pushed her heart back into her chest where it belonged. Shooting a quick look at the open doorway, she saw Mari Bingham standing on the threshold staring at her with a small smile on her face.

"How long have you been there?" Lily asked.

"Long enough to know that the secret to good PR is to talk to yourself," Mari said, and came into the room without waiting for an invitation. She plopped tiredly down into one of the chairs opposite Lily's desk, and, as she was wont to do whenever she had the chance, Mari lifted her legs and crossed her ankles on the corner of the desk.

One of Lily's eyebrows arched. "Tired, are we?"

"Oh," Mari said, leaning her head back as she waved one hand at Lily, "don't go all Miss Perfect Etiquette on me now, Lily. We *both* know you prop your feet up all the time."

"My desk, my feet," she pointed out, smiling.

"My clinic, your desk, my feet."

Lily laughed. "Fine. You win."

Mari smiled but didn't open her eyes. "Thank you. God, I needed this break. I've had two deliveries since 3:00 a.m. and one miscarriage. My feet think I've forgotten how to sit down."

"You're young," Lily quipped. "You'll make it."

"I may make it," Mari said on a sigh, "but if Bryce has his way, I'll be playing doctor at the women's prison."

"You don't believe that for a minute."

"Don't I?" Mari lifted her head, opened her eyes and looked at Lily. "I can't really count on anything anymore when it comes to Bryce," she admitted. "I mean, I used to know him, but…"

Lily watched worry streak through Mari's eyes, and she spoke instinctively to quash it. "Your father just said to me last night that times change—people don't. Bryce is still the man you know. He's just…"

"Being a jerk?"

"Male, really, but in this case, it amounts to the same thing."

Mari smiled briefly and a few of the shadows in her eyes lifted. "Thanks. I'll try to keep that in mind."

"Good." Lily started stacking the papers on her desk, then picked up her pen to make a note to call the caterers about the fund-raising dinner.

"So, Dad told you that last night, did he?"

She stopped writing.

Lily's grip on the gold-plated pen tightened until she was almost surprised that the black ink didn't come squirting out the top of the darn thing.

Carefully she lifted her gaze to Mari's and found the younger woman watching her with a knowing gleam in her eyes.

Well now, Lily thought. Here it comes. She'd known going in that there could be trouble. Having an affair with her employer's father was possibly *not* the best career move she might have made. But even as she thought that, she admitted to herself that whatever happened, last night had been worth it.

She'd never felt such overwhelming sensations. Never been touched with so much fire and tenderness. Never known the incredible joy of sharing a bed with a man who was determined to make you the climax queen of the South.

Oops. Better keep those particular thoughts buried just a bit deeper when talking to her lover's daughter.

"Enjoy Big Jim's, did you?" Mary asked casually, linking her fingers atop her abdomen.

Lily's eyes narrowed on her. "How did you—"

"Please." Mari laughed shortly. "That little piece of news had spread all over town before you and dad got your dinner check."

"But it's an hour outside of town."

"You've never heard of telephones? We have them down here, too, you know."

"Oh for heaven's sake." Someone in that restaurant had obviously spotted Ron and her and hadn't been able to wait to get home to start the rumors buzzing. She should have expected it. After all, it was a small place. Not much to gossip about—until lately, at least. And maybe people were looking for a change of pace. Get tired of trying to convince your neighbors that Mari Bingham was a closet drug dealer? No problem. Here's a juicy little nugget just picked up at Big Jim's Barbecue.

"So, did you two have fun?"

Lily leaned back in her chair, folded her arms across her chest in the age-old image of self-defense and looked at the younger woman opposite her. "What did your sources have to say about that?"

"*Oooh.*" Mari grinned and wiggled both eyebrows, clearly enjoying herself. "Apparently you two were seen dancing close enough that a marriage license wouldn't have fit in between you."

"Oh my…"

"*And,*" Mari said, dragging that one-syllable word out into at least three or four.

"There's more?" Lily winced, wondering just what was going on in Mari's mind about all this. Hard to tell when the woman was so busy teasing Lily.

"Oh, yeah. Gets even better."

"Of course it does," she said on a sigh.

"It seems that dad's hand slipped down onto your…'bee-hind,' I believe was the word."

"For pity's sake." Lily felt a blush rise up and fill her face with heat and color. This had to be a new record. A woman her age blushing.

"And I'm assured," Mari continued, "that you approved of the maneuver."

"Oh, God." Lily sat forward, folded her arms on her desk, then dropped her forehead on top of them. Small towns, she reminded herself. This was what she'd wanted. To be a part of a place. To have everyone know her.

Well, what was the old saying? "Be careful what you wish for?"

"So, did you?"

Lily lifted her head briefly to glare at Mari. "Did I *what,* exactly?"

"Enjoy it, of course." Mari's legs dropped to the floor and she sat up in her chair, leaning her own forearms on the desk as she stared directly into Lily's eyes. "Did you want Dad to—or did you tell him to knock it off?"

"Your report was apparently unclear on that?"

"The spy was interrupted by the arrival of her dinner. She had to hang up before I got the full details."

"At least I'm spared something then," Lily muttered.

"So tell me."

"Why would I?" Lily asked warily. "You're not only the man in question's daughter, but my employer, as well. Remember?"

"The reason I want to know is *because* I'm his daughter," Mari said, and the teasing light was gone from her eyes. Now when she looked at Lily, she was dead serious, though her eyes shone warmly. "Do you like him?"

"Mari—"

"Come on, Lily. Be a pal."

She blew out a breath and frowned. But she admitted, "Yes. I like him." She wasn't willing to say more on that subject, however. Surely it was bad enough that she'd admitted to *herself* that she loved the very sturdy, very attractive Ron Bingham. She certainly wouldn't be spreading the news far and wide.

It would be enough to have Ron running for Outer Mongolia.

"I'm so glad," Mari said softly.

"What?"

"Glad." Reaching across the desk, Mari laid one hand on Lily's forearm. "Dad's been alone too long, Lily. He loved my mom…we all did." Her eyes went dark and damp for a moment, but thankfully it didn't last. "But she's been gone for ten years. I don't want to see him alone for the rest of his life."

"Oh, Mari," she said, shaking her head and sitting up straight. "Don't get your hopes up in that direction."

"Why not? You said you liked him. And I can *tell* he likes you."

"Liking and spending the rest of your life with someone are two very different things."

"Yes, but it has to start somewhere, doesn't it?"

"You of all people should know that what you feel for someone isn't always enough." It had been said kindly, and Lily really didn't want to hurt Mari by reminding the woman that she *had* walked away from Bryce, the man she loved. But she could see in Mari's expression that she'd made her point. "Sometimes things just don't happen the way you'd like them to."

"And sometimes," Mari countered, pushing herself to her feet with a tired groan, "if you want them badly enough, you can *make* them happen."

Lily stood up, too, just to keep things on an even keel. The daylight pouring through her office windows only defined the fatigue on Mari's face, the pale-purple shadows beneath her eyes. Lily's maternal instinct...the one she'd never been allowed to use...kicked in as she came around her desk and wrapped her arms around her friend.

"Instead of worrying about your dad and me," she said softly, "why don't you start taking better care of yourself. You're going to worry Ron if you don't get rid of those suitcases under your eyes.''

Mari's lips twisted briefly, but she nodded. ''I *am* tired. Maybe I'll go into the back room and take a nap.''

''Good idea. We'll call you if we need you.''

Mari nodded and started for the door. She stopped at the threshold though and glanced back over her shoulder. ''I mean it, Lily. I'd really like you and my dad to be happy together. I think you'd be great for each other.''

''Thank you, Mari. That means a lot to me.''

Warmth flooded Lily, stealing her breath and making the threat of sudden tears a very real possibility. But she blinked them back and told herself it didn't matter if Mari was in favor of a permanent relationship for her father. All that really mattered was that Ron was still in love with the woman he'd lost ten years ago.

And though he might have room for sex in his life...he didn't have room for love.

The Bingham home on the outskirts of town was impressive. Lovely, yet hardly palatial, it had stood in the same spot for generations. It now held a settled, comfortable look, as if well pleased with itself.

Ancient trees lined the yard, and flower beds were meticulously weeded and pruned. Hydrangea bushes, showing off the last of the flowers for the season, huddled along the line of the house and brightly cheerful impatiens hugged the bases of the trees.

Lily pulled into the long drive and shut off the engine of her snazzy little red two-seater convertible. She stared up at the house and was, for some bizarre reason, reluctant to go inside.

Fine, she thought, rebelling against her own cowardice. She knew exactly why she didn't want to go inside. She'd already had a heart-to-heart talk with her lover's daughter. She wasn't entirely sure she was up to a repeat performance with the man's mother.

But, she couldn't very well sit out in the car all afternoon. So, deciding she would be the consummate professional, Lily grabbed her camel-colored leather briefcase and climbed out of the car.

Smoothing her short, straight red skirt, she plucked her suit jacket off the back of the passenger's seat and slung it carelessly over her left shoulder. It was too hot to wear it, but she liked to have it nearby, reinforcing the supremely confident-career-woman image.

"You're being ridiculous, you know," she muttered to herself as she took the short set of steps that led to the wide front door. "Myrtle is a lovely woman who is interested solely in the fund-raiser—and she has every right to be kept apprised."

So why then did she feel like she was walking into the Inquisition?

She rang the doorbell, waited two seconds and then the door was being opened—by Ron. Ridiculously enough, she felt like a teenager who'd just bumped into the boy she had a crush on. Her heart jumped and skittered wildly in her chest, and she was pretty sure her blood pressure had just taken a soaring leap toward the heavens.

Lily swallowed hard and looked up into his blue-green eyes. "I didn't expect to see you here."

"I can tell," he said wryly. "You don't exactly have a poker face, Lily."

"Good thing I've never played then, isn't it?"

"As I recall, you're actually pretty good at games," he murmured, one corner of his mouth tipping up into a wicked reminder of last night's intimacy.

In seconds her memory picked up the thread of what he was talking about. At one point they'd actually done a little role playing. She'd played the part of a saucy waitress to his lonely, long-distance trucker.

And it's a new world's record, she thought a heartbeat later, when she blushed for the second time in one day.

As she remembered their night together with an embarrassed smile, she could see the smile slide from his face and develop into a finely tuned scowl. Probably not a good sign, she told herself.

Taking a deep breath, she pushed thoughts of naked Ron to one side and said, "I'm here to see Myrtle."

"Of course. Come in." He stepped back and waved her inside.

She came close enough that her bare arm brushed against his chest, and she sucked in a long gulp of sweetly air-conditioned air, hoping to quell the fires already leaping inside her.

It didn't help.

Ron, though, was apparently having no trouble restraining himself from grabbing her. "My mother's in the front parlor, waiting for you."

She followed him in and told herself not to let her gaze stray down to his backside. But heck, she was only human.

Cool and green were Lily's first impressions. The room was very much like Myrtle in that it was stylish while being welcoming. Elegant and yet comfortable.

She spotted the elderly woman—though she'd never use that word aloud to describe Myrtle Bingham, as she suspected it might be worth her very life—the moment she walked into the room. Ron's mother was perched on a dainty, floral-fabric sofa, with an antique, Wedgewood china tea set on the low table in front of her. Two chairs had been pulled up opposite the table, and Lily dropped into one of them.

"Thank you for coming, Lily," the older woman said.

"My pleasure," she answered. It really was, though it might have been more comfortable if Ron hadn't been present. Hard to face a woman when you were imagining her son naked.

"If you don't mind, I'll just pour the tea while we talk," Myrtle said in her quiet, cultured voice. Hospitality had been born and bred in the woman, and she smiled even while she ordered, "I'd like to hear your final plans for the fund-raiser."

"Of course." Lily fumbled in her briefcase and mentally cursed her suddenly uncooperative fingers for their inability to pluck the one paper she required from the folder within. Finally she snagged it and pulled it aloft like a victory flag.

Shooting Ron a surreptitious glance, she read off a few of the figures and ideas she'd set into motion and then accepted the hot cup of tea from Myrtle.

"It's a good idea, I think," the older woman said as she lifted her cup and took a dainty sip. "Ron, what are your feelings?"

Ron, with his size and overt masculinity, looked like the proverbial bull in a china shop. Immensely out of place in the clearly feminine room, he nonetheless picked up his teacup and took a sip before answering his mother.

Avoiding meeting Lily's gaze, he said, "I'm sorry to disagree, but I don't think an 'old-fashioned county fair' is the right way to go."

"Really?" Stung, Lily looked at him and waited for an explanation.

He frowned slightly but didn't bend. Turning to face her, he said, "I know you've worked hard on these plans, Lily, but don't you think we should be holding the fund-raiser at a nice hotel? Say in Lexington maybe?"

"Oh, what a clever, original, *boring* idea," she said, a little hurt that he'd take a shot at the plans she'd been working on for weeks.

He straightened as if jabbed in the back with a poker. "I'm trying to be reasonable," he ground out, giving his mother a quick glance before continuing. "Which of these patrons are going to be willing to drive all the way out here to give away money?"

"None of them if all we offer is another chicken à la king dinner," she said, and heard the snap in her tone too late to stop it. Hurt and angry, she shifted her gaze from Ron to Myrtle, knowing that in the older woman she already had a formidable coconspirator. "If we make this fun, the people will come. We'll give them a chance to play carnival games for great prizes. They can buy raffle tickets for a chance to win a new car. There'll be ice cream and watermelon and hot dogs and cotton candy. It'll be an end-of-summer celebration." She sent Ron a long look. "And they *will* come."

"But in Lexington—" he began to argue.

Lily cut him off, ignoring the fact that Myrtle had been about to jump into the conversation. "They don't need to see Lexington. Most of them live there. They need to *see* the clinic. The research facility."

His scowl deepened.

She took a breath and said, "Ron, there's been a lot of bad press lately. People are worried. Some of our long-standing supporters have already pulled away. We've got to get these people down here to look over the place for themselves. They've got to *see* with their own eyes what a wonderful job the clinic is doing. How fabulously up-to-date and modern our hospital and school are. And just how much good that research facility will do for not only our little corner of Kentucky, but the world."

The silence rang when she stopped speaking.

Several long seconds ticked past as she stared at the man who, only the night before, had kissed every inch of her body. There was distance between them now. The very wall she'd felt going up the night before now shimmered in between them with an invisible strength.

She wanted him to believe her.

Wanted him to trust her to pull this off.

And it surprised her just how *much* she wanted his faith.

"Well, Ron?" Myrtle said after the silence had stretched to impossible lengths.

He didn't take his gaze off Lily as he answered, "I still think it's a risk."

"But—" she said.

"But—" he interrupted her neatly. "I guess this is why Mari hired Lily in the first place. For her expertise. Her business sense in the PR game."

"True," Myrtle said, her interested gaze sweeping from her son to Lily and back again.

"And the bottom line is," Ron added, "I may think it's wrong—but Lily says it'll work. And I believe her."

Lily released a breath she hadn't been aware of holding. He believed her.

It wasn't quite the same as believing *in* her.

But in a pinch it would do.

"Then we're in agreement," Myrtle said decisively, and Lily shot her a quick look in time to see a small, secretive smile curving the older woman's lips. "And now that we've finished our little discussion, why don't we indulge ourselves in the delicious cakes my cook has prepared for us?"

As Myrtle passed a delicate, pink-rosebud-covered plate laden with iced finger cookies and tiny, hand-decorated cakes, Lily studied Ron from the corner of her eye.

Whatever there was between them hadn't been settled.

And she had no idea where this was leading.

But as long as she was already on the road, so to speak, she would enjoy the journey until it ended.

There was always time for pain...later.

Chapter Twelve

Sunlight sifted through the trees, tracing lacy shadows across Myrtle's manicured front lawn. A warm breeze carrying the scent of pines slipped past the couple strolling down the drive, then hurried along the road as if racing to make an appointment. Birds and squirrels sang and chattered from the tops of the trees, and in the distance traffic roared faintly, like a bored lion.

"My mother called this morning, asked me to be here for your meeting," Ron said as he walked Lily to her car.

"I was sort of surprised to find you here," she said.

He nodded, but didn't look at her. Instead he kept his gaze fixed on her small sports car in the driveway. "I...meant to call you earlier today."

She laughed shortly. "No, you didn't."

He stopped dead and turned to face her. "What?"

Lily sighed and looked up at him, squinting slightly into the afternoon sunlight. Another slap of wind pushed past them and lifted her blond hair into a wild twist around her head, reminding him of how it had looked the night before, stretched across his pillow.

"You didn't know what to say to me," she said, "so you didn't say anything."

"Know me pretty well, do you?"

She gave him a small smile that looked more sad than amused. "Well enough to know that you're not quite sure what to do about me."

Oh, Ron knew what he wanted to do. He wanted to pull Lily into his arms and hang on tight. To recapture the magic he'd discovered with her only a few short hours ago. But it was broad daylight now, and dreams only came at night.

"Lily..." What was he supposed to say? How could he tell her that she was right? He didn't know what to do next. Should he go on with Lily and take whatever happiness with her he could find? Would that be fair to her when he didn't know if he could give her any more than he already had?

But she didn't wait for him to stumble around looking for the right words.

"Don't worry about it, Ron," she said, turning toward her car again. "I told you going into this that I'm a big girl. We agreed on an affair, remember? Not a *love* affair."

Ron thought he'd seen a flash of pain in her eyes just before she turned from him, and he hoped to God he was wrong. He hadn't meant to cause her grief. His hand at her elbow, he tried to ignore the slipstream of heat sweeping from his fingertips up the length of his arm to center in the middle of his chest. Just touching her, even through the fabric of her white silk blouse, was enough to remind him of touching her more intimately. More deeply. And he wanted it again.

After taking her home in the small hours of the morning, Ron had retreated to his condo, and the silence in the place had shouted at him. More than before, the rooms echoed with emptiness. He kept hearing Lily's laughter, feeling her warmth, recalling her sighs.

He'd been more alone after Lily left than he had been in ten long years.

Those first few months after Vi's death, he'd thought he would never laugh again. Thought he'd be lonely for the rest of his life. Slowly, eventually, he began living again, but always, *always,* Vi had been in the back of his mind. The memory of her sweet face, her slight figure, her quiet smiles and gentle nature.

Those memories had become a part of him. He'd kept them close, needing only to shut his eyes to bring his late wife back to him. To feel her in his heart as she'd once filled his life.

But now...

Ron swallowed hard, and his fingers on Lily's elbow tightened perceptibly. Now those precious memories were being supplanted one by one—by images of Lily.

And he didn't know if he could allow that.

Bryce Collins braced his elbows on top of his cluttered desk and propped his head in his hands. The headache that had been his constant companion for the past few weeks had doubled its efforts to make him miserable.

It was working.

The pain behind his eyes throbbed and pulsed in time with his heartbeat. A mountain of aspirin wouldn't be enough to soothe this pain away. He'd be carrying it as long as the ax was hanging over Mari's head.

Grumbling to himself, he pushed away from his desk and walked across the station house floor to the coffeepot in the far corner. Caffeine probably wasn't the best idea when your head was exploding, but if he was going to die, he'd die happy.

"Almost happy," he corrected a moment later after taking a sip. Cop-shop coffee was legendarily bad. But this brew gave a whole new meaning to the words *rotgut*. Thick and black with an oil slick on its surface, the coffee was bad enough to punish.

And since he figured he needed a little more punishment, he took a deep swallow and grimaced as the hot liquid slid down and hit the pit of his stomach like a balled fist. Outside his office, the Binghamton Sheriff's Department hummed with activity. It was a small outfit, made up of only a few full-time deputies and a couple of part-timers Bryce could call in case of emergencies or big events.

They weren't big city, but Bryce was proud of his team and of the work they did. The work he'd devoted his life to. Which was only one of the reasons it was so difficult for him to deal with Mari—the woman he'd once loved more than life itself—as a potential suspect in a drug case.

"Damn it," he muttered around another hideous slurp of coffee, "why won't she help me on this? Why would she fight me even now?"

Because she was obstinate, hardheaded, stubborn… "Beautiful."

He jerked and shook his head, preferring to pretend that he hadn't heard himself say that aloud. Mari wasn't his anymore. Now their relationship was all business. Sheriff to suspect. The way it had to be.

The phone rang, and he stalked across the room toward his desk, grateful for the interruption. He snatched the black receiver and snarled, "Collins."

"Hey, bro!"

That's perfect, Bryce thought. Since he already had a headache, why not add his little brother to the mix? "Hello, Joey."

"Dude, what's with the bad attitude?" Joey's voice sounded high, full of fun and attitude.

And a part of Bryce wondered what he was on. Drugs this time? Or just drunk?

"Sorry," he said. "Just busy around here. What's up?"

"Can't a guy just call to talk to his big brother?"

He probably could, Bryce thought, but Joey didn't usually call unless he wanted something.

"Sure," he said, unwilling to get into an argument with Joey and just too damn tired to play any games. "What's new?"

"Only the greatest thing ever," Joey said, his voice crowing. Then he rushed on, words tumbling over each other in his rush to talk.

While Joey rambled, Bryce dropped into his desk chair and leaned back, staring up at the water-stained ceiling tiles. Practically a new building, he thought, disgusted. Have to call maintenance in and have them check out the water pipes in the courthouse rooms above his office.

"You'll see, bro. It's all coming together."

"What?" Bryce straightened up and frowned. "What's coming together?"

Joey sighed dramatically across the phone line. "Dude, you weren't listenin'."

"Sorry." He wasn't, not really. Hearing Joey's drunken ravings wasn't one of his favorite pastimes. And with everything else he had on his mind, Joey's wild schemes were not high on his list of priorities.

"I *said*," Joey repeated, his voice even more slurred now than it had been when he'd first started talking. "I got a plan."

"What plan?"

"Perfect, bro. Perfect. I'm gonna get rich and screw the Binghams all at the same time."

Man. What was left of Bryce's patience dried up. Joey had been singing the same song for years. According to him, the Binghams were responsible for everything from the high price of gas to ants ruining a picnic.

"Right. Great. Look, Joey, I gotta get back to work."

"Okay," Joey said quickly. "But you just wait, bro. It's all gonna be great. Really soon. You'll see."

"That's good, Joey. You take it easy, okay? Lay off the booze for a while."

"Right. Right. Hey, bro. Don't worry 'bout me. I can handle my liquor."

"Sure you can, Joey."

When his brother hung up, Bryce stared at the phone receiver for a long minute, before laying it back in its cradle.

Family could really make you nuts.

Lily opened the back door and waved a kitchen towel at the roiling cloud of black smoke lifting from her stovetop. The smoke and the scent of charred steak flew out into the yard to dissipate in the soft, evening wind.

"A good thing your neighbors are used to you, Lily," she muttered. "Or there'd be a fire truck pulling up in your driveway right about now."

Her eyes stinging, she kept waving the towel in the smoky kitchen, chasing the last of the billowing black clouds out the open doorway. Disgusted with herself, she shot an angry glare at the now warped broiler pan, sitting atop her stove. And on that pan was what was left of her filet mignon, now about the size, color and consistency of a charcoal briquette.

"So much for dinner," she muttered and tossed the kitchen towel onto the table. She pulled out a chair and sat down heavily.

From the living room came the soft sounds of smooth jazz, drifting from her stereo as cool and haunting as the evening breeze sliding down off the mountain. Through the open kitchen window, she could hear her next-door neighbors laughing and talking as they barbecued what smelled like heaven. And here, in chez Cunningham, she thought with a sigh, one tasty baloney sandwich coming right up.

But she wasn't even hungry.

Her stomach was twisted into so many knots, Lily was fairly sure she wouldn't be able to choke down a bite of food. By trying to prepare a steak, she'd been trying to convince herself that everything was normal. As it should be. But it was pointless.

What was the use of lying to yourself?

Her world *wasn't* normal.

And it probably never would be again.

Ever since leaving Myrtle's house, she'd been remembering Ron. Standing beside him in the shade of the old trees, she'd almost been able to *feel* his confusion. His indecision.

Her heart ached at the memory, and she felt foolish. For heaven's sake, she'd known going into this that Ron didn't—*wouldn't*—love her. His loyalty, his affection, were still with the woman he'd married and lost.

Nothing had changed.

So why, then, did she feel so…disappointed?

"Lily?"

A deep, familiar voice called her name, and everything in her quickened. Her pulse skipped happily, and her heartbeat thundered in her ears. Apparently, knowing that you were being foolish wasn't enough to correct the situation.

She straightened up in her chair and shot a look at the empty doorway leading to the living room and the open front door beyond. Lily was already pushing up from her chair when Ron's voice came again.

"Lily, are you all right?"

Walking through the kitchen and the shadow-filled living room, she kept her gaze on the screen door, where Ron stood silhouetted against the twilight.

It shamed her to admit how her palms went damp and her mouth went dry as she approached him. Didn't seem fair somehow, that she could be so affected by his presence, knowing that he didn't feel what she felt.

She stopped a foot from the screen door and asked, "What're you doing here?"

He glanced around at the yard and street, as if making sure no one was observing him, before looking back at her. "Wanted to see you."

Her idiotic heart that didn't know enough to protect itself against further injury leaped in her chest. She fought it back down. "Why?"

"*Why?*"

She nodded. "Simple question, really."

He shoved one hand through his usually neat, now

rumpled, hair, then shoved that hand into the pocket of his black slacks. "Can I come in to talk about this?"

Come in, she thought, away from prying eyes and nosy neighbors.

"Afraid to be seen at my door?"

"If I were," he pointed out, "I wouldn't be here at all, would I?"

"Good point." Ridiculously, she felt better, just acknowledging that he'd risked gossip to see her. And for a man like Ron, that was saying something. She stepped forward, unhooked the latch and pushed the door open. "Come in."

She turned and walked into the living room, more to keep a safe distance between them than to guide him into the house. After all, her place was small, cozy she liked to think. But with Ron standing so close behind her, the room seemed to shrink considerably in size.

She turned the switch on the nearest lamp and banished the shadows to the farthest corners of the room. Golden light pooled over the table and flowed over the rich colors of the Turkish carpet covering the gleaming wood floors. She looked up at him and saw that golden light reflected in his eyes. It seemed to wink at her, despite his solemn expression.

"Everything okay?" he asked, his voice rumbling into the strained silence between them.

"Why wouldn't it be?"

"When I pulled into your driveway, I saw smoke."

Lily groaned and perched on the back of the over-stuffed sofa. "That was just me. Cooking."

His mouth curved slightly, and she scowled at him.

"Finally," he said. "Something you're not good at."

One of her eyebrows lifted into a dangerous arch. "Well, now that you've been reassured that my house isn't burning down…"

"You must be hungry," Ron said quickly, ignoring the implied request that he leave. He couldn't leave her. Not yet. All he'd been able to think about all day was being with her. And now that he was here, he wasn't ready to go.

"Not really," she said, pushing up from the sofa and starting for the front door. "I'll make a sandwich or something."

"We can do better than that." He snagged hold of her upper arm as she walked past him, and then he led her through the house toward the kitchen.

"Really, it's not necessary—"

He stepped into the kitchen, winced at what was left of the steak, then dropped her arm and headed for the refrigerator. "Everybody has to eat, Lily."

"Ever hear of a drive-through?" she asked. "Or takeout?"

"Cooking's easier."

She snorted. "Depends on your point of view."

He looked at her over the open door of the fridge. "We all have our strengths."

"And yours is?" she asked, dropping into a kitchen chair.

"Omelets," he said, stepping away from the refrigerator, holding an armful of ingredients.

"You cook?"

"I'm no chef, but yeah." He set everything down on the counter and started assembling what he'd need. Glancing at Lily, he said, "You can slice the peppers and onions."

She stood up, sighed and reached for a knife.

He stopped her. "You *can* slice without taking off a hand, right?"

She gave him a tight, unamused smile. "Not my *own* hand, anyway."

"Ouch," he said, laughing. "I'll consider myself warned."

Minutes ticked past as they worked in silent companionship. Ron had missed this. The simple time spent with a woman in the kitchen. Doing everyday, mindless tasks. The teamwork that sprung up between a couple without their even having to try to find that balance.

Hell, he thought. Be honest.

He'd missed *Lily*.

He hadn't stopped thinking about her for longer

than a minute since the previous night. And seeing her this afternoon at his mother's house had only churned up the need building inside him. He hadn't expected this. Hadn't counted on *need*. He'd thought only of *want*.

Now his heart and mind were at war with his body, and he had no idea which was going to win.

"I wouldn't have thought you'd be much of a cook, either."

Lily's voice, calm, quiet, startled him and he glanced at her. "Why?"

She shrugged. "From everything I've heard about your late wife, I can't imagine you were left to your own devices very often."

Ron stiffened slightly, then forced himself to relax.

But she noticed. Sighing, she said, "Never mind."

"No," he said. "It's okay. Stupid not to talk about Vi since she was a part of my life for so long." And if it felt strange talking to his lover about his wife, then he'd just have to deal with it. "Vi was a busy woman. Charitable functions, meetings, volunteering. There were lots of nights I was left to forage in the kitchen."

Funny, he hadn't remembered that in years. Whenever he remembered their marriage, he recalled it in Technicolor snapshots of perfection. He'd selectively forgotten the little annoyances that plagued all relationships. He'd created a gilt-edged memory that shone brighter with every careful recollection. When had he started this subtle process of revisionist history? When had he stopped remembering Vi the woman and created Vi the icon?

"Independence is a good thing," Lily said.

"Yeah," he said quietly, still thinking about his little discovery.

"Ow!"

Her sharp exclamation had him dropping his own knife and turning toward her. She was holding her left index finger and watching blood well up from the neat slice she'd just made across her own flesh.

Grabbing her hand, he dragged her to the sink, turned on the cold water and held her finger under the icy stream.

"That hurts!" she complained from behind him as she tried unsuccessfully to pull her hand free.

"Not surprising," he muttered, even as he tightened his grip, turned off the water and then elevated her hand to stop the bleeding. Looking at her, he asked, "You're not a big bleeder, are you?"

Her mouth twisted. "I only bleed as much as necessary."

"Good to know." He kept a firm hold of her hand and pulled her closer to him. "You should be more careful."

"No lectures, thanks," she said, trying to push away from his body.

"How about a bandage instead?"

She sighed, surrendering to his ministrations. "In the bathroom."

"Where?"

She directed, he led and, once at the bathroom, he slathered antibacterial ointment on the cut, then wrapped a bandage tight around it.

"Do I need stitches?" she asked, staring at her injured finger.

"No, just some tender loving care."

Her gaze shot to his. "You have someone in mind for the job?"

Ron stared down into her dark-brown eyes and felt himself falling, tumbling helplessly into those soft, warm depths. "Oh, yeah."

She swallowed hard, but didn't struggle when he pulled her tight against him. "Are you sure?"

His gaze moved over her even as his hands stroked up and down her back, defining every curve, every line of her body. "Never been more sure."

"You weren't this afternoon," she said, and he saw again the hurt in her eyes.

He lifted one hand to stroke the side of her face, letting his fingers slide into her hair at her temples. Like silk, he thought, and wondered at the cool slide of it across his skin.

Blowing out a deep breath, he admitted, "There's plenty I'm not sure about Lily." He felt her stiffen slightly, but a little pressure on her bottom melded her to him until she felt his body's reaction to her nearness. "What's between us confuses the hell out of me. But, damn it, I'm not ready to walk away from it."

He paused, looked down into her eyes and tried to let her see everything he was thinking, feeling, when he asked, "Are you?"

Her beautiful eyes glimmered with the sheen of tears as she reached up, pulling his head down to hers. "No, Ron. I don't want to walk away."

"Thank God."

Chapter Thirteen

The pain in her finger forgotten, the pain in her heart ignored, Lily gave herself up to the wonder of Ron's kiss.

His mouth came down on hers hungrily, fiercely. With lips, teeth and tongue, he claimed her physically as he hadn't been able to emotionally. Wrapping his arms tightly around her, he lifted her off the floor. Lily clung to him, digging her fingers into his shoulders before sliding her hands down his back. She felt his muscles tighten and bunch beneath the fabric of his cotton shirt.

He tore his mouth from hers, gasping for air like a dying man. "Bedroom?"

"Oh, yeah."

He grinned. "Where?"

"Oh!" Lily dropped her head to his chest and chuckled. "Out the hall, second door on your left."

"Got it."

"Oh, you sure do," she said, clinging to him as he carried her on the brief walk to her bed.

His long legs made short work of the trip. In seconds they were in her room, and Ron sat down on the mattress, still holding her tightly to him. His mouth took hers again, but this time, though the hunger was there, she also felt control and strength pouring from him.

She wrapped her arms around his neck and shifted so that she was sitting astride his lap. The black skirt she wore hitched high on her hips. Groaning softly, Lily let her head fall back as she felt his erection pressed to her center. Instinctively she rocked her hips, moving against him, increasing the mounting pressure for both of them, feeding the need rising within.

"What you do to me," he whispered into the curve of her neck as he tasted her pulse point, flicking his tongue against her skin in rhythm with the pounding of her heart.

She speared her fingers into his hair, loving the feel of his mouth on her. His beard roughed her skin, making the sensations more pronounced, more...vibrant.

"You do the same to me," she whispered, eyes closed while she let him feast on her.

His hands slid from her hips to her thighs, and she shivered in anticipation. Still rocking her hips, she felt his fingertips against her heat and groaned in frustration as he met the fragile lace of her panties—a barrier between them, but not for long.

He snapped the elastic with a quick twist of his wrist and she smiled as he snatched the fabric and tossed it aside. "You're going to owe me *lots* more lingerie."

"I'm good for it," he mumbled as he reached to stroke her.

"Ahh..." The word came out on a sigh. "Yes, you are." She lifted into his hand, wanting him to touch all of her, explore her depths and take her back to the mountaintops.

One finger, then two, dipped inside her, and Lily nearly whimpered. She went up on her knees, wanting more, needing more. She wiggled against his hand, squirming under his touch and delighting in every caress. On and on he went, teasing, torturing with a gentle hand. He touched her, and she went up in flames. He stopped, and she wanted to weep. She needed him as she'd never needed anyone else. She wanted him with an all-consuming strength that shattered her.

She *loved* him as she'd never expected to love.

His thumb brushed across her core, and she splintered, whispering his name as the world dissolved into a quivering mass of light and shadow.

And at last, when the trembling stopped and her body had floated back to earth, she settled on his lap again. Looking up into his eyes, she said quietly, "I missed you."

He cupped her face between his palms. "I missed you, too. Desperately."

"Good."

"My house was too empty without you."

She smiled. "Better."

"I had to be with you."

"Better still."

"I want you so much," he admitted on a groan, "I can't think of anything but you."

"Don't think, remember?" she said, reminding him of his own words the night before. "No thinking. Only feeling."

He nodded and dipped his head to kiss her.

While their mouths mated, Lily let her hands drop to his lap. With deft, clever fingers, she undid his belt, then opened the button and zipper on his khaki slacks. He groaned again, tightly, and pushed his tongue into her mouth, sweeping inside her warmth, plunging her into a swirling abyss of desire and passion.

Yet she wouldn't be dissuaded from her task. She freed him from the prison of his trousers and curled her hand around his length. Stroking, caressing him, she felt the strong man in her arms tremble at her touch, and her own sense of completion roared inside her. Sensual power shimmered within, and she gave herself up to the heady rush of it.

He ground his mouth against hers and when she went up on her knees again, his big hands took hold of her hips and guided her to him. Slowly, she sank down, taking him in inch by slow, deliberate inch. Drawing out the pleasure, stoking the fires higher and higher.

Ron broke the kiss and fought for breath. Staring up into her eyes, he watched her expression as she took him within her. He wanted to rush, to dive into her heat and lose himself there. But he also wanted this moment to go on forever. So he let her set the pace. Allowed her to take charge. Forced himself to give up to her. To surrender all that he was and wait for her to accept it.

He sucked air through gritted teeth as she continued her agonizingly slow assault on his senses. His body felt ready to burst. His heart raced and his blood rushed through his ears with a roar that was deafening.

The world came down to her.

To one pair of dark-brown eyes.

To one slightly turned-up mouth.

To one curvaceous, warm-hearted woman holding him in thrall.

Seconds ticked past, measured in small eternities. He gulped in a deep breath of air and held it as she finally accepted his full length into her damp heat. They were joined. Physically. Emotionally.

He felt her heart touch his.

Felt his soul slide from the shadows toward a light that was blinding.

He shifted his hands, drawing them up to the buttons on her blouse. As she sat atop him, he undid the small, pearlized buttons and pushed them free until her white silk blouse hung open, displaying a bra that was more lace than fabric. Hungrily he slipped her blouse off and down her arms, then tossed it aside. Just as hungrily he flipped open the front catch of her bra, and when she shrugged out of it, filled his hands with her breasts.

"Beautiful," he whispered, bending his head to taste first one, then the other. Lips and tongue worked her rigid nipples, and he smiled against her skin when she sighed and dug her fingers into his shoulders. She rocked into him, moving her hips on his body in a slow, sweet slide that pushed him nearer the edge.

He loved her breasts.

Loved the lush, full feel of them in his hands. Vi's breasts had been small, delicate. But Lily had a gen-

erous build that fascinated him and drew him to her
even in his dreams.

He tasted her again and ran the edges of his teeth
across her nipple until she twisted and moaned atop
him.

"Torture isn't fair," she whispered brokenly.

"It is if it's fun," he countered.

"Remember you said that." With that warning, she
reached down and cupped him as she moved atop
him.

"Lily..." He stared at her now, transfixed by the
passion glittering in her eyes. She barely breathed as
she moved on him, up and down, side to side, driving
him wild, driving him higher than he'd ever been before.

"Take me," she murmured, "and let me take
you."

His breath staggered from his lungs. His vision
blurred. His heartbeat skittered.

She rode him with a fierce abandon and pushed
them both to the brink of madness. And when he
couldn't stand it a moment longer, he grabbed her,
pulled her off him and tossed her onto the bed.
Scrambling now for his wallet and the protection he'd
brought along, he took care of things then lifted her
off the bed, holding her hips in his hands and guiding
her down onto his body once more.

She groaned, locked her legs around his hips and

held on. Forgetting about the bed, forgetting about niceties, he backed her up against the wall and drove himself inside her. Need roared, and he answered. Over and over again, he entered, withdrew, then plunged within again. Taking, claiming, accepting.

And when she called his name, tightening around him, he whispered, "Lily," and joined her in the fall.

The next week flew past, and Lily and Ron settled into a routine of sorts.

They didn't talk about it. Avoided mention of it, really. But they became a couple. Lovers. Meeting whenever they could and coming together in glorious bursts of passion that left both of them shattered and wondering what would happen next.

But there were no answers since neither of them posed the question.

Lily stared out her office window and only half listened to the everyday hubbub of the clinic. A dangerous time, she thought. Having caught up on her work, she had nothing to fill her time with except thoughts of Ron. And heaven knew, he was taking up far too many of her thoughts lately.

The affair she'd thought would be simple had become the most important thing in her life. The only problem was she didn't have a clue how Ron felt about her. And she didn't have the guts to ask.

Huffing out a breath, she stood up and headed for

the small kitchen at the back of the clinic. What she needed was a snack. Maybe if her blood sugar was high enough, she could go thirty seconds without thinking about the man she never should have loved.

But the minute she stepped out of her office, she walked into chaos. The front door of the clinic was thrown open and she heard a man shout, "Somebody *help!* She's having a baby!"

Lily smiled at the frantic note in the poor man's voice. In these rooms the husbands and boyfriends were the outsiders. Here women created life, and men could only watch, unable to help, unable to ever completely understand what it was to be a part of creation.

She started for the waiting room, but the anxious couple were already headed toward her and the delivery rooms. Hannah Bingham Mendoza was patting her husband's hand, while Eric was looking blindly around the room with a panic that was nearly palpable. His dark-brown hair was practically standing on end, and his even darker eyes were frantic. Lily'd never seen the unflappable Eric looking quite so on the edge. He spotted Lily and shouted, "Find Mari. Get her fast."

"Relax, now, Eric. Hannah will be fine. We'll take care of her."

"I'm staying with her," he said, and gave her a look that dared her to contradict him.

"No problem," she said, lifting both hands in

mock surrender. Lily spotted Crystal, one of the nurses, standing at the end of the hall. Her strawberry-blond head was bent forward as she studied a picture in her locket. Every line of the younger woman's body screamed with tension. Yet, when Lily called her name, Crystal snapped the locket shut and stood up straight, a forced smile on her face.

"Yes?"

"Tell Mari her cousin's here and ready to deliver."

"Right." Crystal nodded sharply, then sprinted past them down the hall and took the turn toward the hospital wing.

Lily, meanwhile, took Hannah's free arm and caught the eye of Heather, the receptionist. "Why don't you have Eric fill out the papers and I'll take her into the back."

Heather rolled her eyes but nodded. "You got it. Come on, Eric," she said in a soothing, overly patient tone, "do the paperwork while they get Hannah settled."

He glanced after his wife. "But I want to be there."

"You will be. Forms first."

"Can't they wait?"

Heather just sighed, grabbed hold of his arm and practically dragged him back to her desk.

Lily helped Hannah into the closest empty room

and settled her in a rocking chair. "There you go, honey, how're you doing?"

Hannah stroked the mound of her unborn child and smiled. "Better than Eric."

"I got that much," Lily said with a gentle laugh. "He loves you. That's why he's so worried."

"I know." Hannah's smile was wide and dreamy. "Wonderful, isn't it?"

"Yes, it is."

Mari skidded into the room from the hallway, nearly breathless from her dash from the hospital wing. "Hi, kiddo, we ready to party?"

"Oh, yeah," Hannah told her, taking a deep breath and then blowing it out as another contraction gripped her. When it passed, she smiled weakly and looked up at her cousin. "So, is it too soon to demand drugs?"

Mari laughed and helped her out of the chair and onto the bed. "First, let's get you settled."

Lily watched the younger women for a long moment, then said, "I'll go check on Eric and send him back when you're ready."

"Thanks, Lily," Mari said, throwing her a quick grin over her shoulder. "And tell him to calm down, will you? I heard him over in the children's wing."

Love, Lily thought as she walked briskly down the hall toward the waiting room and the nervous father-to-be. It was an amazing thing, really. Love had brought Hannah and Eric together. Love had made them a family. Love had convinced Eric to be a father to a child that wasn't, biologically speaking, his.

Love was the real miracle.

She spent the next several minutes helping Eric remember his phone number, and when Mari signaled that it was time, Lily walked him back to the birthing room. She stood in the hall, unable to leave, listening for that first, magical cry.

When it finally came, a heartbreaking wail that seemed to echo down the halls, Lily smiled and told herself that miracles happened every day.

How could she not hope for one of her own?

The night of the fund-raiser was crisp and cool. As summer ended and drew into fall, twilight came earlier and the stars seemed to shine even more brightly.

Party lights were strung across the grassy divides between the clinic and the hospital. There were game booths, rides, and hot dog and cotton candy stands. All of the people manning the attractions were volunteers from town, wanting to help raise money that would bring much-needed jobs to the county.

Music drifted from the bandstand where a local country band was tuning up and playing a few songs to put themselves in the partying mood.

And in the lobby of the clinic, Ron looked around at the faces gathered there. His family and friends.

His daughter, Mari, looking tired, but happy. His son, Geoff, and Geoff's new wife, Cecelia, fresh off their honeymoon, were practically glowing with love and happiness. Friends he'd known since childhood and a few more he'd been lucky enough to pick up along the way were also there, helping Ron support the research facility that had been so long in the planning.

And then there was Lily.

She moved at the edges of the crowd, smiling, laughing, talking. She did her job well, he thought, and felt admiration swell inside him. She'd pulled it off and, judging from the reactions of the guests who'd already started lining up at the games outside, she'd been absolutely right to go with her "country fair" theme.

She glanced at him and, even from across the room, he felt the impact of her gaze slam home. Flames licked at his insides while he did his damnedest to look cool and professional. He wondered if the people gathered here to toast the fund-raiser had heard the gossip about Lily and him. He wondered what they thought and then asked himself if he really *cared* what they thought.

The answer was no.

Surprise flickered through him, like the winks of light thrown from a kid's sparkler. He'd expected to care. He'd been working hard to keep what he and Lily had found together just between them.

Yet suddenly it didn't seem to matter.

With pride in his eyes he watched her work the crowd and followed her every movement. Her blond hair was swept behind her ears to display long, diamond-studded chains hanging from her lobes. The earrings swung with her energy, keeping time with her steps. Her bright-red dress was cut low enough over her breasts that one of the guests treated himself to an eyeful of her cleavage.

Anger spurted inside Ron, and he wanted to tell the old fool to put his eyes back in his head. But then Lily smiled and moved on, charming everyone. She chatted, laughed and patted hands as she worked the room like a southern politician.

And she had them all…including Ron…in the palm of her small hand.

"Dad?" Geoff said quietly from beside him. "You okay?"

Ron came out of his musings and glanced at his son. Smiling, he said, "Yes. I'm fine. Great, in fact. I was just…thinking."

Geoff smiled sadly. "About Mom?"

Guilt jabbed at Ron's insides. No, he hadn't been thinking of Vi tonight. His thoughts had been centered on an elegant blond with a body designed to make a man crazy. She couldn't cook, but her laughter was food for the soul. She loved to dance, but had two left feet. She was as hardheaded as he was and not too intimidated to stand toe-to-toe with him and argue.

So, no, he hadn't been thinking about Vi at all. And as he looked from his son's understanding gaze to his daughter's smiling face, Ron began to understand why. His children and the life he'd made with Violet were his past. A wonderful time that he wouldn't have changed or traded for any amount of treasure.

But that magical time was gone, and he was left standing at the threshold of the rest of his life. The question was, how would he face the coming years? As a man mourning a love lost? A man afraid to try again for fear of losing once more?

"Dad?" Geoff prodded. "You're zoning out, here. You sure you're okay?"

Ron nodded and sucked in a deep breath. "Yeah. I'm sure." He clapped one hand on Geoff's shoulder and slipped the other arm around Mari's waist as she came up to join them. "Before we go join the party," he said softly, keeping his voice low enough that only his children would hear him, "I wanted you both to know how proud I am of you."

"Dad—"

He smiled at Mari. "I'm *fine*," he said, anticipating her question. "Can't a man tell his kids they're good people without everyone thinking he's dying or something?"

"Hey, I'm convinced," Geoff said, and slapped his

father on the back. "And thanks, Dad. It means a lot to me."

"Good." Ron met his son's gaze and saw with absolute clarity the man he'd become. Pride didn't define the feelings coursing through him. But now wasn't the time for reflection, he told himself as the crowd began to get restive. Now was the time to party and collect enough money to set the research facility on a strong foundation.

He glanced from face to face, smiling at his friends, nodding to acquaintances, before finally landing his gaze square on Lily for a long, thoughtful moment. Even from across the room he felt the threads binding them. This bond with Lily was something he hadn't expected. Something he'd told himself he didn't want.

And yet now he drew on that strength, bathed in the warmth he saw in her eyes and felt…complete.

"Welcome," he announced in a booming voice, demanding the room's attention. As the people turned and looked at him expectantly, he flashed them all a wide grin and said, "What do you say we take you big spenders to the fairground, pry open your wallets and start the party?"

Chapter Fourteen

A week later it was official.

The fund-raiser had been a resounding success.

It seemed that the movers and shakers of Kentucky society liked nothing better than to throw down bundles of money for the chance of winning carnival prizes. The band had kept the crowd dancing until late into the night, and the raffle prizes, everything from a weekend at a hotel in Lexington to a brand-new car, had been a huge hit. People in town were still talking about it, and the financial backers of the research facility were as happy as those financial types ever were.

In the quiet of her office, Lily smiled as she ran the last of the figures on her calculator. She hit the total button, grinned, then leaned back and enjoyed the sweet, proud glow that settled in her chest. And it wasn't just the amount of money raised but the satisfaction of a job well done that had Lily silently congratulating herself.

She'd thrown a party that had pleased everyone and done its job. Mari was delighted. The townspeople would be talking about the bash until *next* year's fund-raiser, and Myrtle Bingham thought Lily was a genius.

"Always good to keep the boss happy," she muttered as she lifted her feet to the edge of her desk and crossed them at the ankles.

Now, she thought, frowning suddenly, if only her personal life was running as smoothly as her professional one. Wouldn't that be a happy thing?

But no chance of that.

She and Ron met nearly every night at either his house or hers. They went on picnics and to the movies, split milkshakes at the local diner and went dancing at Big Jim's. And every date ended with the two of them locked in each other's arms, discovering new ways of making magic together.

Lily squirmed on her seat, just thinking about those amazing nights. She'd found more with Ron than she'd ever known existed. Not even that first rush of love she'd felt for her ex-husband so many years ago could compare to what she experienced just looking into Ron's eyes.

In a few short weeks he'd become so important to her it was almost impossible to remember her life without him in it. He was her last thought before she fell asleep and her first thought on waking up.

No doubt they were the talk of the town. She'd caught the covert glances tossed at her, and more than once she'd spotted Mari giving her an indulgent, nearly wistful look. Even Ron's son, Geoff, now that he was back from his honeymoon, had stopped by twice to see her, both times giving her a warm hug that felt like a welcome to the family. "He's probably been talking to his sister," Lily whispered on a sigh.

But it didn't matter what people were saying or thinking. She and Ron never discussed the gossip or what it might mean. In fact, both of them had become quite expert at talking *around* what really mattered.

Passion, desire, *need* was easy for them.

Flames erupted whenever they came together. Flashes of emotion rattled in the air around them. But the future was never acknowledged, and questions were never asked.

And the invisible wall that stood between them hadn't been breached on either side. Lily couldn't admit her love for him without risking him running for the hills. And Ron wouldn't admit he felt anything for her because it would, or so he apparently thought, take something away from what he'd had with Violet.

Lily pulled her feet down and swiveled in her chair to look out the window at the cloudy skies beyond the glass. Wind whipped through the trees, and she shivered as if she could feel the bite of it slicing into her flesh. Summer was sliding into fall. Changes. Life was about changes.

What didn't change, or grow, died.

The love affair between Ron and her was trapped. It couldn't grow and wouldn't change. With her gaze locked on the treetops, she wondered how long it would be before what she'd found with Ron ended.

She was suddenly cold to the bone—and the weather had nothing to do with it.

"What is wrong with you?" she demanded out loud.

Leaping up, she stalked to the window, unhooked the latch and threw it wide open. Instantly the cold wind swept past her, lifting loose papers off her desk and swirling them onto the floor. And at the same time, the wind scattered her dark thoughts.

She curled her fingers over the windowsill and held on tight. Her mind raced; her heart pounded.

"Since when do you walk away from a fight?" she asked herself in a low, strained whisper that came from her soul. Pulling in a deep breath of that frigid air, Lily stared blankly at the trees and lawn beyond the glass. Outside, nursing and midwifery students were hurrying to their next classes. Expectant mothers were walking arm in arm with their husbands, trying to hurry labor along. And inside the hospital and the clinic, people were working, putting their hearts and souls on the line for what they believed in.

Just as *she* always had.

Stiffening slightly, Lily lifted her chin and shifted her gaze to the cloud-tossed sky above as if she could stare straight into Heaven itself. Then she said in a quiet, firm voice, "What you had with him is over. And you have to let him go. I don't want to fight you, because I probably couldn't win." That was a hard one to admit, she thought, but then, how did one do battle with the ghost of perfection? Still... "I love him. And I'm not going to let what we have end without at least *telling* him so."

Pushing away from the window, she added, "If you have a problem with that, I'll be outside in a minute. Find a lightning bolt."

Ron stood in his mother's front parlor and wished he didn't feel like a kid again, being called on the carpet for shooting birds with his BB gun.

"Don't look so damn nervous," his mother said, waving him into a chair. "For heaven's sake, Ron. I'm not an ogre."

"Since when?" he asked wryly, one eyebrow lifting into an arch.

His mother's lips twitched in amusement. "Fine, then. I'm an ogre. So do what I tell you."

"Not gonna be here that long, Mom."

"Then say what you came to say." She reached for the flowered teapot to pour herself a second cup.

"Right to business, huh?"

"I'm too old to waste time," she said, then took a sip of her favored Earl Grey. After she'd swallowed, she added, "As are you."

His mother had always been honest, he thought, scraping one hand across his beard. And hadn't he been thinking the same damn thing for the past few weeks? That he was too old for the foolishness of starting an affair? Of enjoying an affair? Of *needing* someone as much as he'd come to need Lily?

"But when do you get too old for love?" he wondered, and didn't realize he'd asked the question aloud until his mother answered.

"Who says you do?"

"I'm sorry?"

She set her teacup back into the saucer with a gentle clink of fine china. Putting them both onto the tea tray, she stood up and crossed the room to the wide front window, looking out over the expanse of yard.

Ron watched her and felt a flicker of admiration. His mother was still what used to be called "a fine figure of a woman.'' Tall and straight, she spoke her mind with an innate sense of grace and style that always seemed to bring out the best in people.

''You're never too old for love, son,'' she said quietly, her back to him as her gaze locked on something only she could see.

He frowned to himself. He hadn't meant for this to become a deep discussion. In fact, he wasn't even sure why he'd come to his mother's place. He should be at work. Hell, he couldn't even remember the last time he'd left the office in the middle of the day. But he simply hadn't been able to concentrate on anything.

The business couldn't hold his attention.

Nothing could.

He felt restless, uneasy. And no matter how he tried to steer his brain in another direction, inevitably, his thoughts focused on Lily and how soon he might be able to see her again.

Just a few short months ago, he hadn't known her. Now he couldn't imagine *not* knowing her.

He'd gone into this affair with what he'd thought was a clear head. He hadn't wanted love. Hadn't wanted to care, even. But Lily had moved into his life, his heart, his mind. She was a part of him now in a way that he hadn't experienced in far too long.

And he liked it.

Which only made the guilt crawling inside him even stronger.

His mother sighed. "Do you really think that because the body grows older, the heart does, too? It doesn't. It still loves, it wants, it needs. It *breaks*." She glanced at him over her shoulder, smiled fondly, then turned her gaze back to the trees lining her wide front yard. "Age means nothing, Ron. Age is a state of mind— No. Wait. It's not a state of mind, it's a state of *soul*."

"What?"

She laughed softly. "If you're able to feel, you must feel. That will keep you young, always. If you close yourself off to emotion, to change, you wither and your soul dies—then, you become *old*."

"Well, that's cheery," he said. "Thanks, Mom."

She turned to look at him, and the afternoon sunlight shone around her silhouette like a nimbus of gold. Smiling, she said, "That's not what you wanted to hear?"

"I wasn't looking for philosophy," he said, shoving both hands into his slacks pockets.

"What were you looking for, then?"

"I don't know." Shaking his head, he strolled across the almost dainty room to stand beside his mother. "Confirmation, maybe?"

"Of what?"

He glanced at her. "Lily."

"Ah…" She smiled and nodded regally.

Really, he thought, his mother would have made a good queen. "That was a knowing 'ah.'"

"Mothers know everything, don't you remember?"

She certainly had when he was a boy. He'd never been able to get away with a thing. And for a long time he'd been convinced his mother was a psychic. But all mothers were like that, he'd discovered. Vi had been.

Vi.

He stiffened.

Myrtle stared at him for a long minute before saying abruptly, "If she's making you unhappy, I'll be happy to fire her."

"What?"

"Lily," Myrtle said, walking back to her seat on the sofa, so that her pleased smile would be kept hidden from the confused man who was her son. "I said I'll gladly fire her for you."

"That's not necessary."

"Are you sure?"

"Mother."

"She is an annoying woman, after all."

His tone surprised, he said, "I thought you liked Lily."

Myrtle shrugged and busied herself with picking up her teacup again. "She's served her purpose. And she *is* a stubborn woman, isn't she?"

"She's just...opinionated."

"But she argues with you."

"Only when she believes in what she's saying."

Myrtle hid another smile as she took a sip of tea. "I hear she can't even cook."

"Cooking isn't that important." Ron stared at her as if he'd never seen his own mother before. He couldn't believe what he was hearing. She'd never in her life said an ugly thing about anyone as far as he knew. And to start now...with Lily, of all people. "You can't cook, either, remember?"

She waved that comment aside. "And, she's very...different, wouldn't you say?"

Anger flickered to life inside him. Ron stalked across the room toward her in a few long strides. "What's that supposed to mean?"

Myrtle met his hot stare with a cool look. "She's very unconventional. Always sticking her nose into things."

"Trying to help, you mean?"

"Plus, she's so very different from Violet, don't you think?"

He yanked his hands from his pockets, threw them into the air, then let them slap hard against his thighs. "What difference does *that* make?"

"Why," Myrtle said innocently, "I don't know, dear. What difference does it make to you?"

"Not a damn bit of difference," he snapped. In

fact, he loved that Lily was so different—not only from Vi but from anyone he'd ever known. With Lily he was never sure what was going to happen next. And, for a man who'd lived most of his life on a tight schedule, that feeling was damn near invaluable.

"But didn't you prefer your life before Lily came here and shook everything up?"

Before Lily? Sitting in the empty condo at night, wishing for someone to talk to? To dream with? To laugh with? Going through his days with a resigned sense of emptiness and the sure knowledge that all of the good times in his life were already gone? He choked out a harsh laugh. "God, no."

"Really? Fascinating," Myrtle said, and set her cup and saucer down again before carefully selecting an iced blueberry cake. "Still, if I see that she's fired, life will become so much...*easier,* don't you think?"

"What's easy about having nothing but work in your life?" He heard his voice getting louder and louder but he couldn't seem to stop himself. For God's sake, he'd expected his mother to understand. She'd always believed in the power of love, affection and loyalty.

"Oh, it's so much simpler, dear. Love is so messy, you know." She lifted one hand to her mouth and gasped prettily. "Sorry. It isn't as though you love Lily. My mistake."

His mother's wide, innocent eyes looked up at him,

and for the first time since this ridiculous conversation had started, he noticed the glint of sparkling amusement.

Ron opened his mouth, then snapped it shut again. Drawing his head back, he looked down at his mother through narrowed, thoughtful eyes. She'd played him like a pro. She'd insulted Lily until he'd defended her. She'd made him face his real feelings. She'd forced him to see that Lily was far more important to him than he'd been willing to admit.

"Has anyone ever told you what a sneaky woman you are?" he asked, bending down to kiss her soft cheek.

She patted his face gently and gave him an understanding smile. "Not since your father died," she said. "So thank you."

"No, Mom," Ron said. "Thank *you*."

Then he straightened up and headed for the door.

"Where are you going?" she called out after him.

He stopped in the doorway. "There's one more person I have to talk to before I can talk to Lily."

As he left, Myrtle leaned back against the plush sofa cushion. Smiling to herself, she whispered, "Say hello to Violet for me."

The clouds lowered, and the wind kicked up with a vengeance.

Walking through the cemetery just outside Binghamton, Ron was struck, as always, by the history of the place. Generations of people buried here. People who had laughed and loved and lost. People who'd found the beauty in life alongside those who had never opened their eyes to it.

And the question he had to answer now was, which did he want to be?

His footsteps were sure on the rolling green grass. He faced the onrushing wind, ducked his head and walked on, not needing to think about his direction. He'd been here so many times, he could find his way in the dark. And had, more than once, in the first few months after losing Vi.

He'd come here looking for solace, but had never been able to find it. Ron knew in his heart that Vi wasn't here. Had never been here, really. She'd moved on ten long years ago.

Now it was time for him to do the same.

He sighed as he stopped in front of the simple, pink granite stone.

Violet Stephens Bingham.

She'd died too young. Only forty short years on earth and yet she'd managed to make them all happy ones. Wasn't that saying something special about the woman he'd once loved so completely?

Shoving his hands into his pockets, he stared down at the plot of neatly trimmed grass, decorated with a spray of fall flowers. Gold and red chrysanthemums dipped and swayed in the wind as if dancing to a tune only the angels could hear.

"Hello, Vi," he said softly, knowing his words would carry to the woman who would always be listening for them. "It's been a while since I've been here to visit. I'm sorry for that."

Guilt chewed at him, but he didn't give in to it. His late wife would never have expected him to devote himself to visiting her grave. That had been his idea. He'd found a solitary refuge here in the quiet garden of stones.

A refuge he didn't need anymore.

Lifting his gaze from her headstone to the swirling dark clouds overhead, he pulled in another long, shaky breath and said, "I wanted you to know, honey, that I think I finally understand what you meant that last night. I didn't want to hear your words then, Vi. And for a long time I just refused to remember them."

He sighed and looked again at her name carved in stone. "But I get it now. Do you remember? You said, 'Love, Ron. Live and love.'"

Smiling, he crouched in front of the granite marker so that he was on eye level with the carving. Reaching out, he fingered the dancing flowers, as if by doing so he could touch a memory of Violet. "I'm ready to love again, Vi. Thanks to you, I know what that means. It means living. Continuing. And thanks to you, I'll always treasure every moment I have here on this earth.'' His fingers dropped to the cool, sweet grass and he gave the ground a gentle pat, as if in farewell.

"I'll always love you, Vi. That won't stop.'' He stood up again and looked down solemnly. "And that's the real beauty of love, isn't it? It doesn't end. It only changes.''

And in the quiet swirl of wind, Ron said goodbye to his past—so he could say hello to a future.

Chapter Fifteen

Lily vacuumed, dusted, then scrubbed the kitchen floor. She did laundry, then waxed the floor when the overloaded machine spit an ocean of suds at her. She tuned the stereo to an oldies rock and roll station and worked in time to the music that acted as both a soother and an energy boost.

She needed both.

Since leaving her office a few hours ago, she'd tried to keep busy. To keep her mind from settling on what was sure to be an explosive confrontation between her and Ron. Her insides twisted at the thought of confessing her love and having to watch him walk out of her life.

But some risks were worth taking, she told herself firmly. She wiped down the kitchen counter for the third time, then turned and scowled at the pot on the stove. Steam billowed from under the lid even as white, foamy liquid boiled over the sides and dripped down onto the stovetop.

"Damn it." Rushing across the room, she grabbed at the lid of the pot only to drop it with a clatter and bring both burned fingers to her mouth. "For God's sake, Lily, are you *really* that pitiful?"

Snatching up a kitchen towel, she wadded it up and used it as a hot mitt to lift the lid and inspect the cooking rice. Giving the contents of the pan a stir, she frowned at the soupy mix and the white kernels floating aimlessly through the murky liquid. "It's *rice* for Pete's sake. It's not a soufflé!"

But it didn't seem to matter.

She checked the box and reread the directions. One cup of rice, one cup of water. She looked at the coffee mug she'd used to measure it all out. One cup. Should have been simple. So why wasn't the quick-cooking rice quickly cooking?

She never should have tried to fix dinner, she told herself in disgust. Should have just bought something. Would have been safer. But then, there had been a small voice inside her whispering that maybe if she could convince Ron that she wasn't totally helpless in the kitchen, she wouldn't come off quite so badly in comparison to the late, great Violet.

"Stupid." She dropped the lid onto the stove, turned the fire off under the pan and took a step back from the damn thing. "If he wants a cook, he can hire one. I never pretended to be anything but what I am," she continued and flashed a glance heavenward, disregarding the ceiling that stood between her and the object of her conversation. "Okay, fine. I admit I'm lousy housewife material. But I *love* him, doesn't that count for something?"

"Depends," a deep voice answered.

Lily jumped, shrieked and whipped around to stare at Ron, standing in the doorway. "Are you trying to kill me?" she shouted, hoping that her heart would drop back into her chest before it choked her.

"Nope."

"Could have fooled me, sneaking up on a person like that in the middle of a private conversation." Great, she thought. Good start to the evening. An argument. Well then, maybe if they fought hard enough, it wouldn't hurt so much when he leaves.

Liar.

"Just who were you talking to?" he asked, walking into the room with the slow deliberation of a man who had all the time in the world.

"Not that it's any of your business," she snapped, "but I was talking to Violet."

One dark eyebrow lifted. "Really? Funny, I was just doing that myself."

She laughed shortly, but there was no humor in it. "I'm not surprised."

"Don't you want to know what I said?"

Lily tipped her head to one side, folded her arms across her chest and adopted what she hoped was a casual expression. "Do I want a play-by-play of you chatting with your dead wife? Let me think." She paused a beat. "No."

Shut up, Lily. Shut up.

Her temper, the very one she'd been trying to work off all afternoon, was still with her. It wasn't all anger, either. It was a defense mechanism, pure and simple. She knew it. She just couldn't seem to stop it.

Basically she was staying angry with him so he couldn't hurt her.

It was an old game.

But one she was very good at.

"Too bad," he said, taking the single step that put him within an arm's reach of her. "Because I'd love to know what *you* were talking to Vi about."

Her mouth worked as she tried to remember exactly what she'd been saying as he entered the kitchen. Had she been complaining still? Or had he heard her confess her love? And if he had, why was he still here and not running for his car?

"It was private."

"Then you shouldn't shout."

She winced, and her anger evaporated, leaving her shaken and worried and way too anxious about saying the words she'd been rehearsing all afternoon. "Probably not."

"What's that?" he asked, jerking a thumb at the pot on the stove.

She sighed. "It was *supposed* to be chicken and rice."

He took a step and looked into the ugly mess. "There's no chicken in there. And I'm not sure you could call that rice, either."

Lily laughed. She couldn't help it. Waving her arms in the air, she admitted, "You're right. I suck at cooking. Never wanted to learn."

"So why'd you try tonight?"

She blew out a breath that ruffled the hair that had fallen across her forehead. "I was...trying to prove something, I guess."

"To whom?"

"You. Or maybe, Violet."

He gave her a small smile. "Prove what?"

Lily shook her head and chuckled helplessly. "That I could be a good wife. Of course, you can see the results, so what I succeeded in proving was just the opposite."

"A wife?"

She looked up at him and was astonished to see that he hadn't backed into a corner like a caged animal. "Don't worry, that wasn't a proposal."

"Good."

"Well you don't have to be so happy about it,"

she muttered, tossing the towel she still clutched in one fist at the kitchen sink.

"Why shouldn't I be?" he asked, still smiling, still watching her.

She stared at him for a long minute, then told herself, What the hell, and let him have it. "You shouldn't be happy because I'd be a darn good wife. Okay, I can't cook. And I can't have children, but I wouldn't want any at this stage of my life, anyway." She held up a finger when he opened his mouth to speak. "But I'm a good person. And I'm fun and loyal and loving. I could make sure you don't keep yourself locked into a beige, boring world. I could make you happy, Ron. As happy as you could make me."

When she ran out of breath, she stopped, but before he could say anything, she took another lungful of air and sped ahead. "And there's one more thing. I *love* you, you big dummy."

Both of his eyebrows lifted, but she paid no attention.

"That's right," Lily said, walking right up to him until she could poke her index finger against his broad chest. "*Love*. With a capital *L*. I hadn't counted on it. And I know you don't want to hear it, so feel free to run screaming from the house, but before you go, I want to make sure you know I mean it. I love you. More than I ever thought I could love anyone."

"Lily—"

"I know you'll always love Vi. And you should. I don't mind sharing you with a woman who had your heart first...but I won't fight a ghost for you, Ron. You're allowed to love both of us, you know. *And* I won't pretend anymore that I'm happy with the relationship we have. Because it's not enough. I don't want to settle for crumbs if I can't have the whole cake." She sucked in another deep breath and added one last thing, since she was on a roll. "Violet's gone, Ron, and she isn't coming back. I'm *here*. And *I* love you, too."

When she would have continued, Ron shut her up the only way he could think of. He grabbed her, pulled her close and kissed her, long and hard and deep, until his body felt the fire and he knew hers did, too.

After several long, amazing minutes, he came up for air and stared down into her dazed, dark-brown eyes. "You finished?"

She nodded and licked her lips.

"Good. It's my turn."

"Just say goodbye and go, then," she said quietly.

His fingers tightened on her upper arms. "*My* turn, remember?"

"Right."

"I told you I went to talk to Vi."

She nodded.

"I told her about you. I told her that I *love* you. Then I came to tell *you*."

Lily blinked against the rush of tears filming her eyes. "Ron—"

He shook his head. "Still talking."

"Right." She smiled, though, since so many of their conversations went like this.

"I wasn't looking for love again, Lily." His gaze moved over her tenderly. "I figured I'd had my chance, my happiness. Then you blew into town and turned everything I've ever known upside down."

She smiled. "It's a gift."

"Damn right it is." He shifted his hold on her so he could cup her cheek in the palm of his hand. He had to touch her. To feel the amazing jump of connection that leaped between them. Then, sighing, he said what he felt, for the first time in years. "Vi was my first love, Lily. She always will be. But *you* are my *last* love. She was my past, *you* are my future. And I'd like to be yours."

"Ron…"

"I came here to propose, but your ambush threw me off."

"Pro—"

He reached into his jacket pocket and pulled out a small, dark-green velvet jewelry box. Lily inhaled sharply as he opened it and showed her the star sapphire and diamond ring inside. "Marry me, Lily. Dance with me. Sing with me. Argue with me. And love me as much as I love you."

He slipped the ring onto her finger, and Lily's hand

closed around the platinum band as if trying to hold it on even closer.

Lily looked down at the perfect stone and stilled, as if everything within her had taken one long breath and paused. This was a moment she wanted to remember. A moment she wanted to be able to pull out of her treasure trove of memories and visit again and again.

This was, at last, the one moment when she'd found the man she was meant to love.

Finally she lifted her gaze from the ring of promise on her hand to look into the blue-green eyes that had become so important to her. She looked deeply and read the emotions she'd wanted to see for so long. His love was there, out in the open, shining for her.

There were no more shadows.

No ghosts standing between them.

And that invisible wall had somehow, incredibly, tumbled down.

"I'll marry you," she said softly, staring up into his eyes, with her heart reflected in hers. Just saying the words made her heart race. "And I'll even let you teach me how to cook."

Ron grinned, swept her into his arms and buried his face in the curve of her neck. His deep, rolling laughter warmed her right down to her soul. "*I'll* do the cooking—and gladly—if you'll promise to dance with me every night before dinner."

Lily pulled back far enough from him that she

could reach up and cup his face between her palms. Her shiny new ring winked at her in the kitchen light and warmed her right down to her soul.

Smiling up at him, she said softly, "We'll eat out—and we'll dance every night for the rest of our lives,"

"Now that's the best deal I've ever been offered," he said, bending his head to claim the first of their new lifetime of kisses together.

* * * * *

Don't miss the conclusion of
Merlyn County Midwives!
IN THE ENEMY'S ARMS
by Pamela Toth
Silhouette Special Edition #1610
Available May 2004!
And look for AND THEN CAME YOU
by Maureen Child.
Coming in July 2004
from St. Martin's Press.

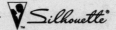

If you enjoyed what you just read,
then we've got an offer you can't resist!

Take 2 bestselling love stories FREE!

Plus get a FREE surprise gift!

Clip this page and mail it to Silhouette Reader Service™

IN U.S.A.
3010 Walden Ave.
P.O. Box 1867
Buffalo, N.Y. 14240-1867

IN CANADA
P.O. Box 609
Fort Erie, Ontario
L2A 5X3

YES! Please send me 2 free Silhouette Special Edition® novels and my free surprise gift. After receiving them, if I don't wish to receive anymore, I can return the shipping statement marked cancel. If I don't cancel, I will receive 6 brand-new novels every month, before they're available in stores! In the U.S.A., bill me at the bargain price of $3.99 plus 25¢ shipping and handling per book and applicable sales tax, if any*. In Canada, bill me at the bargain price of $4.74 plus 25¢ shipping and handling per book and applicable taxes**. That's the complete price and a savings of at least 10% off the cover prices—what a great deal! I understand that accepting the 2 free books and gift places me under no obligation ever to buy any books. I can always return a shipment and cancel at any time. Even if I never buy another book from Silhouette, the 2 free books and gift are mine to keep forever.

235 SDN DNUR
335 SDN DNUS

Name	(PLEASE PRINT)	
Address	Apt.#	
City	State/Prov.	Zip/Postal Code

* Terms and prices subject to change without notice. Sales tax applicable in N.Y.
** Canadian residents will be charged applicable provincial taxes and GST.
    All orders subject to approval. Offer limited to one per household and not valid to
    current Silhouette Special Edition® subscribers.
    ® are registered trademarks of Harlequin Books S.A., used under license.

SPED02   ©1998 Harlequin Enterprises Limited

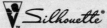

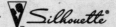

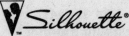
Silhouette®

COMING NEXT MONTH

SPECIAL EDITION

#1609 TREASURED—Sherryl Woods
Million Dollar Destinies
Artist Ben Carlton didn't believe in an enduring love. After all,
he'd lost the ones he loved the most. So he took refuge in his
work…until he met gallery owner Kathleen Dugan. The pixie
beauty brought sunshine into his darkened world. But could she
convince Ben to trust in love again?

#1610 IN THE ENEMY'S ARMS—Pamela Toth
Merlyn County Midwives
The last thing Detective Bryce Collins needed was to go soft on the
prime suspect in his investigation. But he and Dr. Marigold Bingham
shared a past—and a love—that haunted him still. He couldn't
imagine Mari as the culprit…but was Bryce thinking with his head or
with his heart?

#1611 AND THEN THERE WERE THREE—Lynda Sandoval
Logan's Legacy
Single dad Sam Lowery needed a nanny, not a love interest. But
in Erin O'Grady he got both. Their attraction was mutual…as was
their unspoken vow to ignore it. Living under the same roof gave their
relationship a powerful intimacy. Ignoring lust was one thing,
denying true love was another.…

#1612 THE HOUSEKEEPER'S DAUGHTER—Christine Flynn
The Kendricks of Camelot
Addie Lowe knew her place. Growing up as the housekeeper's
daughter at the Kendrick estate, she could only admire the tall,
dark and delicious Gabriel Kendrick from afar. Social conventions
prevented anything more. But then he kissed her—an unforgettable,
scorching, spontaneous kiss—and it changed everything!

#1613 THE STRONG SILENT TYPE—Marie Ferrarella
Cavanaugh Justice
He wasn't much on conversation. But police officer Teri Cavanaugh's
new partner, Jack Hawkins, sure was easy on the eyes. Teri resolved
to help Hawk come out of his shell. As she did, she couldn't help but
fall for the man he revealed himself to be.…

#1614 FOR HIS SON'S SAKE—Ellen Tanner Marsh
Angus was up to something. Single dad Ross Calder's seven-
year-old son was hostile and unresponsive, unless he was in the
company of one Kenzie Daniels. Ross found himself continually
wrangled into inviting the free-spirited Kenzie to join them. The child
was clearly smitten…but would his romantically jaded dad
be soon to follow?

SSECNM0404